FINDING MAGGIE'S BLISS

A Novel by
Augustus G Van Slyke

Books by author

Book I - DIGGING UP BONES

Book II - FINDING MAGGIE'S BLISS

ANGELS NEVER LIE - Memoir

Disclaimer:
This story is fiction. All characters, places and situations come from the author's imagination. Any similarities of characters are pure coincidence which unfortunately protects the guilty.

ISBN 13: 9780978568931
ISBN 10: 0978568931
Library of Congress Control Number: 2013920310
Lord & Daniels Publishing Incorporated
Scottsdale, AZ

For Judy -
my Sister

CHAPTER ONE

Scottsdale, Arizona - August 2001

A loud commotion woke the ten-year-old. His heart pounded. A shot rang out. A bullet crashed through the small bedroom inner wall just above his head, smashing the mirror on the far wall.

"Stop!" he heard his father shout. Richard slipped out from under the sheets and grabbed his gun. Two more blasts sounded from the room next door. He heard a moan. Then an ominous silence filled the air.

Seconds later he peered through a crack in the door. A stranger leaned over his father with a gun to his head.

Richard's instincts kicked in. He held his new handgun with both hands, just as his father had taught him. Then he aimed, squeezed the trigger, and pumped all nine shots in his 22 High Standard pistol into the back of the intruder...

***

Eighty-one-year-old Richard Fleming wiped the sweat from his forehead with his sopping wet white handkerchief.

His thoughts had shifted aimlessly these past few days. He wasn't feeling well, and the nightmare from his youth never escaped him, its memory forever etched in his mind.

The rusted air conditioner vibrated in the window, blowing in warm air as the glass rattled. The old psychiatrist got up from his desk and trudged to the windowpane. Squinting, he focused on the outdoor thermometer. One-eleven in the shade. "I'll be damned," he moaned as he turned and labored back to the swivel chair at his desk.

He hated the monsoon season; even if it lasted only a few weeks, it was too damned long. The humidity took its toll on the aging doctor.

But now he had another problem to contemplate. He wasn't looking forward to his first and only client of the day. *Damn you, Margaret Lynne Hornsby!* He wanted to help, but liking the woman was impossible. She made it that way. Frustrated, he pushed the leather-bound appointment book aside, picked up his unlit Cuban cigar from the clunky glass ashtray, and stuck it in his mouth.

The old swivel chair creaked as he leaned back and peered at the framed photos, medals, and citations that lined the walls. *"For God and country,"* read one of them, though there were days, like this one, when the former FBI agent felt that God and country had nothing to do with it and he had been in it for the prestige. *Whatever. I'd do it all over again.* Why not? He was proud of his work. He knew how to keep a secret. And how to lie. The government paid him well.

He had been a professional in all the right ways. He'd saved and mended lives. It was his job. And, too, there were times when he had to take lives. If one is to play the game, one plays it to win. There is no other way.

At the beginning, when Richard Fleming was young, he wasn't full of American pride. If he was full of anything, it was questions: Why do people hate? Why do people love? Why do they kill? He was simply interested–obsessed, even–in what made people tick. So he studied and became a psychiatrist. In his youth he was a bookworm. His father, Henry, wanted him to expand his horizons and enjoy the outdoors, too.

So Henry took his son to their cabin in the woods to learn about nature. That he did; he learned about the dark side of man.

Henry had given him a pistol for his tenth birthday. They practiced with it the day before the incident, when a man broke into their summer cottage in upstate New York. That night Richard's father died in his arms from gunshot wounds. A kid grows up pretty fast after something like that, he often mused.

Two years after the tragedy, Richard was twelve and confirmed in a traditional Catholic confirmation ceremony blessed by the bishop of the diocese. He chose the name Francis after Francis of Assisi, a saint he had always admired, and not just because his life was dedicated to helping the poor and downtrodden, as honorable as that may be; it was rather his courage to walk a different path than most. St. Francis left his rich father and joined the army, an act of bravery. And, toward the end of his life he willingly received the stigmata. That was a true act of loyalty.

After the ceremony everyone filed into the church basement for refreshments. The Bishop had too much wine. That night, his mother, Patricia, was driving them home when a car sideswiped them. Forced off the road, she hit a tree.

Richard never got so much as a scratch. Patricia's neck was broken. She died at the scene. An investigation of the hit-and-run accident followed and the driver of the other car was found. It was the Bishop who had confirmed Richard. He was never charged–with anything.

Richard believed in himself and that was enough. He could bullshit an Eskimo into buying an ice cube then, and now. Fuck the rest.

The plaques, trophies, and medals were for the old guys, the survivors. *The best of the best, as they say.* Ironically, he had become one of them.

He loved to look at himself–back then, when he was young and thin. Well, thinner. It didn't matter, the extra weight made him look regal, astute, dignified, even if it was only in his own mind.

He thought of one of his oldest friends, the skinny one, who for all the world reminded him of Barney Fife.

Mickey Zaugbaum could never keep his shirt tucked in-always a half a step ahead of the others, and in a different direction. *I'll be damned if the sonofabitch wasn't right. Always! Damn him to hell.* He worked outside of the organization, contracted himself out, and never made a mistake.

And then there was Mickey's sidekick. Richard loved him, though he drove him crazy! Gordon Maxwell was a thick guy, red-haired and sly, a Sheriff Andy Taylor-country-boy kind of guy. If one thought at first meeting that he was mentally slow, he'd be wrong. He made a lot of people wrong. They paid for it, sometimes with their life. And that was the oddest thing, because he didn't believe in carrying weapons.

Gordon was a sheriff at one time, back when he was young and single (well, single since his wife had left him) and he drank too much.

He was a strange case. Mickey had set up an appointment for Gordon and Richard became his therapist. Gordon was overworked and stressed from a tough assignment. He knew Maggie and a boy named William when they were kids in distress. They had to be saved. He did his job.

Gordon was convinced that William, a fourteen-year-old boy he had protected from family abuse, could fly. He listened, took notes, and asked questions. Gordon poured his heart out from the couch. Richard didn't know whether to laugh or cry at first. He listened to the wild and wacky story. He didn't laugh. And they became fast friends.

Gordon insisted that he take one last patient, and that was when Maggie (as she preferred to be called) walked into Richard's life.

She was trouble from the get-go. She'd tried suicide and her life was a mess. It didn't start out that way. She had good parents—a good life by all standards. Lived in the country and was happy until ... until what?

Richard had worked many a case, but this one ... this one gave him fits. He found himself bolting upright out of bed. It gave him a feeling he'd never felt before. Defeat.

An eerie feeling remained. He couldn't shake it, or his thoughts of his client. *Damn her to hell, that woman! Why can't she see what's right in front of her?*

An object bulged in his pants pocket. Fighting his too-tight pants and driving his fat hand in to it, it ripped. He swore. Pulling it out, he pushed the damn thing onto his desk. Texting. What'll they think of next?

I'm too old to learn new fucking tricks. He thought of Gordon before turning his thoughts to the new nurse, latest nurse, of Doctor Betz. A peculiar woman, yet, he found her strangely exotic. Butch? Maybe. It didn't matter if M.G. swung one way or the other. He treated her like a father would a daughter. She had guts. He liked that.

His eyes were as old as he was. Cell phone keypads were small and harder to see–harder still to hit the right buttons. Technology was making gadgets smaller. *It's not fair for guys my age.*

The damn things are used to set off bombs. Stephen King doesn't even own one. The technology troubled him. But there it was, staring him in the face; looking right back up to him as he looked down at it.

He'd been having trouble with a lot of things lately. Depression? Sure. Richard was getting forgetful, and he knew it. Food had lost its taste and his sense of smell was going. Things that used to arouse his senses, like newly cut grass, burning leaves, bacon sizzling in the frying pan–it just wasn't the same anymore.

And he couldn't do a damned thing about it. Even cigars had lost that crisp taste he had once found so pleasurable.

Like an old retired greyhound, his races had been run. He relived them now as old dogs do–in their dreams.

There was one more case to work on, but Maggie was trouble. Always had been. Years went by, and he couldn't help her, couldn't fix her. He had one more shot. One more note to take, one more statement, once more he would plead with her. And then he had to drop it.

"Talk my thoughts out loud, they told me. So, out loud I do. I'd just fat-finger the message anyway, but what the hell–for old time sake, I'll give it a try. Move, fingers. Are you paying attention, Gordon?"

CHAPTER TWO

Tuesday 2:47 PM - August 2001

That afternoon the two of them went at it.

"Revisit your past, Margaret," he demanded. "It's the only way out!"

She thought, *Piss on doctors! What the hell do they know? So they went to school, partied, drank, smoked dope, and screwed until their eyeballs fell out. All of the higher learning experiences paid for by their filthy rich parents. These so-called psychiatrists don't know shit from Shinola. Boorish fucking bastards! My heart's fine. It beats.*

Where is my daughter? The scars of the past had healed. She was certain of that. The ovarian cancer was killing her. Dr. Betz, her medical doctor told her so.

Dr. Fleming said to Margaret Lynne, "Healing comes from the inside out, *and* it begins with your heart if you are to have any kind of closure at all.

"Write it down," he said. "Write it all down. Throw it up and puke it out. It doesn't matter how you do it so long as you *do* it. Not-one-other-goddamn-thing matters, neither survival techniques nor unending searches for contentment. How *did* you arrive at this point? Intact? Hardly!

"I say there's something missing, perhaps as little as three days. You say there isn't. There's unfinished business and that's a fact. You can't tell me what it is! You've closed off that part of you, a segment of the past, maybe your soul.

"I've tried my damndest but you're a stubborn woman. This journey is all yours, kiddo, bought and paid for upfront. You purchased it in advance the day you were born. Your walk has not yet ended.

"Doctor Aaron Betz, your *latest* internal medicine doctor, and I are in agreement. I've seen the x-rays. The type of aggressive cancer that you have and the prescriptions he and I have given you, should keep you pain-free. Probably for several weeks, a month or two at best."

He had deep reservations about Betz, though he didn't tell Maggie that. After all, he'd been wrong before. He was a fine judge of character–or had been when he was younger, and before his drinking became more than a habit.

Maggie shifted her thoughts to Aaron Betz's aide, the sixties survivor, free-spirited nurse named Morning Glory, M.G. for short. What a hoot. She gave a few select cancer patients a special remedy for nausea she called "Mary." *Short for Mary Jane,* Maggie presumed. "Mary" came in two forms, brownies or rolled cigarettes.

Morning Glory was the name she preferred after taking a drop of speed-laced LSD. She was up for twenty-eight hours. That was in the sixties at the University of Wisconsin. Her first name was Lois and she had never officially changed it. At the clinic the patients referred to her as Dr. Lois, MD.

Dr. Fleming continued, "You'll find, in this envelope, prescriptions for depression. You haven't had a psychotic attack since I weaned you off of it–"

"Anything from Dr. Lois?" Maggie asked, interrupting.

Without skipping a beat he continued, "One is Clexa and the other Paxil. If one doesn't agree with you, try the other. If your panic attacks return, I prescribed Ativan. It'll take the edge off. Two will keep you from nausea and vomiting. You have enough medication to kill a horse. Your life is in your hands, Margaret Lynne. I wish you well."

She had bottles of morphine tablets too. She was hording them rather than taking the prescribed doses from Doctor Betz. He had told her they were potent, perhaps too potent for her. Her life was coming to an end, true, but was he tacitly offering her a choice as to how and when to end it?

Margaret thought back to the first time she met Dr. Richard Fleming. She had slashed her wrists. It was a sloppy attempt at suicide. At their first session, he predictably called it "a cry for help."

"Bullshit," she answered back, "I want out." Now he's giving me all the drugs I could've used back then. Back when I found DUH, my second husband at home, in bed with his friend, the parish priest. The marriage had been a total train-wreck anyway.

"If you follow my advice and listen to your heart, you have an opportunity to be at peace with yourself. Get your rear-end to Evergreen Meadows, the special AA meetings with the guest speaker I told you about, and find yourself, Margaret. *Just this once,* do it my way.

"Alternatives? Take the easy way out if you wish. Swallow the goddamn pills.

"You said gardening is therapeutic. You told me so, once. *It's a healing time of meditation,* you say. Well think of suicide this way; pushing up daisies is therapeutic. You'll be in a meditation garden forever more.

"Everything I've done, all the hours spent with you; the notes taken, prescriptions written, advice given, all of it will have been for naught. My work with you is done. The sessions have come to an end. I wish you well."

She didn't like his comments about suicide. Margaret took the envelope with the prescriptions, folded it, and stuffed it in her burlap bag. They hugged. She felt a genuine feeling of honesty from the big man. She hugged him back saying, "Thanks for everything, Doc, but with all due respect, do one more thing for this old patient. Close the door when I leave, and forget me."

Margaret walked out of the office on her way to her final retreat.

Well, fuck him. Fuck him and the horse he rode in on, she thought. Her mind was still on the words of the cigar chomping, aging psychiatrist. He uses a cigar as phallic symbol. Her anger had not left. And what kind of psychiatrist would show porn flicks to a client in the name of therapy? Even Aaron Betz didn't fully trust Fleming. He had pretty much told her so.

"You know the FBI had a GPS chip implanted in my neck. Did I ever tell you about that, Maggie? They did it when I retired," Doctor Fleming once said.

They put a chip in retired Greyhounds, too. She kept quiet, that day.

Fleming's fractured inexpensive room oozed of the addictive aroma of expensive cigars. It reminded her of the smell of the old radio in the reading room of her childhood home. It smelled of tobacco, too.

Her father smoked a pipe. She enjoyed watching the smoke rise and flutter upwards on its way to the ceiling and then fade and disappear. Back then Margaret would spend hours visualizing herself, floating upwards and disappearing.

It made little Margaret Lynne Hornsby feel safe, and that all was right in her world. Little did she know how soon her little girl world would end.

Ed and his wife, Helen, lived in the country. They could have sent their son and daughter to school in the city where they worked, yet chose to have them educated in a one-room schoolhouse a few miles from their farm house. They refused to be sucked into the hype of big city school systems.

Margaret's mother, Helen, and father Ed, remained true to each other and never wavered. On the other hand, Margaret lived in cities all of her adult life, both here and abroad, and had been married and divorced twice. She bore two children. Girls. Gave one up for adoption. It was painful, but best for the three of them.

Never go slow. Never look back. That was her creed. Journaling now, she glanced about as she reminisced about her past. How odd, she thought. Never look back? What about her vocation? Maggie's degree was in Anthropology, with a minor in Archeology. Digging up bones, looking back into the past, for what? Answers?

"Fuck answers!" she heard herself say out loud. She sat outside of the quaint Internet café, seated at a white plastic umbrella table. There were tables nearby—people sitting, sipping, and now staring. Folding her laptop and jamming her writing journal and pen into the white burlap bag, she jerked it up and onto her shoulder, and walked past the other patrons seated near her.

"Excuse me," she said throwing back her dark brown shoulder length hair, "I was thinking of my ex." She lied.

CHAPTER THREE

Tuesday August 10, 3:10 PM

T he air was warm and heavy. The average-sized airport was nondescript except for a bi-plane hanging from the ceiling. The locals
hardly noticed it. They never looked up. It was usually raining. It was
a great airport to leave from. Someone called it *The Land of the Frozen
Chosen*. Some never came back.

They think the same. Have many of the same interests, same
foods, same team; everyone dresses alike–in team colors. Mostly dark
Lutherans and Catholics. Some hold secrets–dark secrets. Things from
their past.

She flew into Capital City from Sky Harbor Airport in Phoenix.
Her stomach turned. Maggie didn't like the feeling. It felt like a dark
cloud hanging over her head.

The retreat house, Evergreen Meadows by the Lake, was the only
place her HMO endorsed. Doctor Fleming found it for her and it was
easy on her checkbook.

"The best bang for your buck," he had said.

She could handle the twenty-five-dollar co-pay per night's stay,
and it also allowed her something most precious to her now–time. It
offered a new place to reflect, to journal, to become whole. At least
that's what Fleming had recommended and her damned medical doctor, Betz, oddly enough, had agreed, almost insisted, that she go there.
Time was all she had.

As she was about to climb the concrete steps of the entrance, she caught a glimpse of a long shadow of a car leaving the grounds. Her neck hairs stood on end.

Earlier, the rotund female clerk had told her that her room wouldn't be ready until three, so Maggie left her suitcase and carryon with her at the front desk.

"I'll take care of 'em," the lady with the overdue-for-a-re-dye blond hair and red ruddy complexion said. "They'll not leave my sight. I've never lost a thing here," she boasted, leaning on the front desk on the right side of the entrance. She continued, "The room will be ready by three. If you want to get a bite to eat, just walk up to the front gate and turn left. You'll find yourself restaurants and shops. Yup, just a hop, skip and a jump from here."

It had been a long day already as Maggie peered up over her round rainbow-colored framed glasses at the woman, smiling as she thought, *Eat a bag of shit, lady. You have all the personality of three-day-old road kill. I believe you didn't lose anything here, least of all your virginity. I'm sure it's welded in place with sheets of soldered iron.* Instead, she said, "I appreciate your kindness, Ms., ah—"

"Lena, Lena Lundy, is my name." She looked down at the clipboard in front of her and scanned it. "You're Margaret, correct? Let's see and your last name is, Lynne?"

Maggie stood across the desk from her with one hand up on the straps of the bag on her shoulder as her eyes glanced about the dank marble hallway. She couldn't help but smell the raw fragrance of ammonia, as if the place was just scrubbed clean for her arrival, and said, "Right, both times, dearie."

"You have two first names?" Lena asked.

Observing the tight curls of hair on Lena's head, her tongue engaged before collecting her thoughts, "Let me guess, Lena. Your ancestry is Norwegian, is it not? Your mother was a Catholic, your father, a Lutheran? They couldn't marry in church unless he converted. But he remained a Lutheran and your mother raised you as a Catholic."

Maggie wanted to continue by saying, "They tried pleasing every-one because that was their nature. It was the way they were brought up, yet in the end no one was happy, least of all your parents. They wanted out of the crumbling marriage but the family mores and the teachings of the faiths forbade such a thing. As for you, you went into denial for survival and found yourself in the kitchen. You filled your face with homemade pies and ice cream." She didn't.

With astonishment on her round red, ruddy face, Lena put her hands to her cheeks and said, "How in the world did you know that?"

Stepping toward the front desk and laying an arm on the counter, Maggie whispered, "Wild guess."

The "hop, skip and a jump" turned out to be a six-block hike past cornfields. *Miss Scandahoovian can just hop up and kiss my ever-lovin' ass,* Maggie thought as she reached into her burlap bag for her meds. *Talk about being on the edge of nowhere...*

She found an Internet connection at the Hula Java Café. She spent an hour there and sent an email to her daughter—her first in many months. She'd already sent hundreds of unanswered emails. What was one more?

She felt no physical pain by the time she returned to Evergreen Meadows by the Lake. The sign out front crossed off "the Lake." It was so named because of the five-acre lake in the back. The splendid evergreens now stood proud and majestic over and around a very large stinking mud hole.

The water table was low because the guiltless nearby corporate farmers pumped out all the ground water for irrigation. They blamed the drought.

"So, a mud hole, huh?" Maggie questioned as she asked Lena for a water fountain.

"We have bottled water," she replied. "The water here is undrinkable. We have to boil it first."

Maggie curled a nostril looking over her glasses to Lena. "Neat. How much is the water?

"One dollar. Just one God-bless-America dollar," Lena said with enthusiasm and a big smile.

"I'll take two."

"Okey-dokey. I'll just put it on the tab for the room. We'll let the insurance company figure out if you pay or they pay. There's a small fridge in your room. It has a few items in it for you. It's on the house," she said as she giggled.

Lena leaned forward, fumbled around in a side drawer, and came up with a key.

"Here you are Ms. Lynne. Your room is on the third floor on the right. Your luggage is there for you. It's an end room so you'll have a nice view of the oak and aspens near the entrance."

"Thanks, Lena," Maggie said as she tilted her head back and launched three tablets to the back of her throat, and washed them down with four swallows from her eight–ounce bottle of water, then chugged the rest.

"Uh, just a quick question. As I walked by the front entrance, a dark gray hearse drove by me on its way out of here. The driver glanced at me with cold, steely eyes. It gave me a chill. Somebody die? By the way, I thought you said you'd never lose sight of the bags?"

"Oh ya, Ms. Lynn. I carried them up there myself," she said, astonished at how quick Margaret downed the pills and guzzled the entire bottle of water right there in front of her. "Nobody died today. We got a janitor here by the name of Kurt. Kurt Gunderson. But I don't bother him if I don't have to. You know how men are. They can be pretty cranky if a woman tells 'em what to do. Anyway, he also drives a hearse for the undertaker parlors just up the road from here. "He just came by to pick up his check from last week.

He hasn't been around, though, not for the last couple of days. Don't know where he went." Maggie nodded her head and started down the long marble hallway, hesitated, turned and shot a look back to Lena.

"Yup, we don't have elevators," Lena shouted, leaning her stout chest over the counter in her direction. "And another thing, my mother was the Lutheran, my father the Catholic." Lena's voice echoed throughout the swirling beige and brown marble hallway.

Maggie gave her a slight grin and walked to the end of the ever-darkening hallway. Each step echoed off the marble floor. It sounded as if there were others walking with her as she shifted the heavy burlap bag on her shoulder that held her pills, laptop, and journal. There, she turned to begin her ascent up the three flights of stairs–one step at a time.

The stairwell was dark. She couldn't shake the eerie feeling she got from the hearse driver. A change was taking place and she didn't like it. Her stomach ached. Each upward step she took rang out with an echo. The sound began pounding in her head.

She gripped the solid oak railing with her right hand and pulled herself up to the next step. The ringing became constant. Another step up on the solid marble tile, another echo. The ringing vibrated ever louder. At the landing between the first and second floor, she stopped and caught her breath. A glimpse of something strange flashed in front of her in lightning speed.

Little eight-year-old Margaret Lynne was climbing the steps and she was not alone. There was a cold swirling wind blowing–howling in through open doors and windows. Long black shutters slammed back and forth against the brick walls as the cold air forced its way up and back down through the staircase.

Loud menacing, echoing voices surrounded her. They were garbled, yet strong and agitated. She felt a rumbling from within. Horror engulfed her as the cold, wavering voices emerged as ghostly beings. They pushed and pulled at her. She swayed back and forth from side to side as they edged her up the steps. Every fiber of her hair and skin tingled with fear. Her cold, sweaty hands were tied behind her back. A kerchief covered her eyes.

Out of breath, Maggie leaned forward, banging her kneecap on the edge of a step. Her head was spinning. She felt faint as she winced in pain. "Ouch! Mother-fuck, goddamn it, that hurts!" She slid around and sat down on the step. Pulling the tan pant-leg of her capris up over the throbbing knee, she bent over to look at it. It was tender, and even in the dim light she could see it turning bright pink as she heard muffled voices below.

She moaned, "Oh shit. The voices are back and they heard me downstairs. Damn, that smarts." She rubbed her sore knee before pulling the pant-leg back down.

She slid the bag off her arm and stood up. The golf shirt that she bought in Hawaii a few months earlier needed to be tucked in. She had loved her mini-vacation in Hawaii, yet, somehow, she felt uncomfortable. It seemed as if she was being watched. But why? And by who?

Maggie pressed one hand against the floral brown and black orchid printed shirt, and slid it down and under the capris below her belly button and did the same with her left hand. With the bag over her right shoulder, she moved to her left using that railing, continuing with her ascent.

With each step the agitating echoes began anew. The ringing grew louder. She rested on the second and final landing. Again she regained her breath and courage. Just a few feet away from the top something weird was happening. She paused. Her troubled eyes transfixed on the haunting dark metal door.

A gust of howling wind rushed through the bright slit under the door. A flurry of sparkling particles circled around her face and hair before disappearing behind her. It took her breath away. Maggie's heart was beating at an accelerated rate; her hands trembled with fear. She stood frozen and didn't breathe. It seemed like time was passing ever so slowly. She felt as though her lungs were about to explode.

Gasping, she drew a breath. Still raw with anxious emotion, she brushed her hair back from her face, not turning her eyes from the metal door. For a moment the surroundings seemed strangely familiar. The smell. The sounds. It's all so–familiar. *What is it about this building, anyway?*

With her palms sweating, she braced herself along the rail and took another step. And another. There was no echo now, only the sound of the wild wind rushing, seemingly through her, from the slit of bright light under the door.

One of her dizzy spells was coming on. She clutched the rail with both hands. The ringing was deafening. She closed her eyes tight, but still she was woozy. The acid in her rolling stomach made her more unbalanced. She swallowed the saliva in her mouth. She began breathing deep and slow. Finally the dizziness ebbed, as did the ringing.

Then, from out of nowhere, a male voice slammed into her right ear and spoke in a threatening, husky whisper. *"Your parents will be very angry with you if you die. Do as I say and you won't be harmed, you little sinner!"*

Her eyes glazed as she stared at the door. Her pulse pounding fast, it felt as though her heart was going to explode. The ringing became more intense as the blood vessels in her temples throbbed harder and harder. She released her grip on the railing and teetered back and forth. She tried to breathe, but in her state of panic, it was impossible. The dizziness returned. She looked back again, as the staircase moved, shapes altered.

The lone light bulb blinked and dimmed as it swayed and shot bright rays here and there, and then narrowed into a single light-stream. With her last ounce of courage, she lurched forward. Her head slammed against the metal door.

Maggie's hands found the knob and gripped it tight. Her body slid down as she sat on the landing without taking her hands off the door-knob. Shrill and quivering screams were now coming from the other side of the big scary door as beads of sweat rolled from her forehead.

She looked up at the cold, ugly door and said, "I'm too much for you. You're just a goddamned piece of fucked-up metal."

With her stomach contracted like an angry fist, she took one more deep breath and held it. She leaped up, turned the knob, and slammed her body hard against it. The door flew open this time, exposing the third floor as it banged against the wall.

Maggie slid across hallway floor and lay sprawled face-down against the far wall. There was silence. Her eyes were closed. She dared not move. The howling wind subsided. No darkness. No screams. She just lay on the cool, smooth marble floor catching her breath.

Squinting as she tried to open her eyes, she could feel the brightness of the hallway. She blinked and opened them slowly. *Oh God. Maybe you should take me now and be done with the whole matter. Pills and me just don't get along.*

"Psychotic? Panic attacks?" That's what she said to the psychiatrist. He maneuvered the cigar from one side of his mouth to the other before taking it out and resting it in his stinking plastic ashtray on his desk.

"There's nothing to be ashamed of," he said. "It happens now and then. Anyone can have them, Margaret. Your attacks just happen to be more severe than others. Sooner or later you'll have to deal with them, examine them, pick 'em apart so we can get to the source of the damn things and treat it."

Oh, bite me! Big goddamn deal about a little panic attack. They're back. Today, when I least expect it, I get ambushed by a goddamn, fucking panic attack!

She lifted her head off the cold hard floor. Drops of blood dripped to the marble below. She stared at the pool of scarlet. She also felt a warm sensation at the corner of her right eye. She sat up touching it with her right index finger. With her forefinger she tasted her own blood. Licking it off she dabbed the brow again and again until the bleeding stopped.

Dazed, she said aloud, "Here I sit at Evergreen Meadows by the *mud hole,* having panic attacks and bleeding. I was supposed to heal, not go *crazy* here. Is this the beginning of the end? Is this how I'm going to die?" She looked toward the ceiling and yelled, "Bliss! Why haven't you answered my emails?"

***

Down at the front desk the phone rang and rang. "Evergreen Meadows," Lena spoke between breaths.

"Did she arrive?"

"Yes. And she saw the hearse leaving. According to the letter from her doctor, she won't be here long. Maybe a week or two."

"It won't be that long. Say goodbye, Lena."

***

Maggie picked herself up, grabbed her bag, and shuffled a few feet down the faded pale green hallway. The walls looked like they hadn't been painted since the first half of the last century. The fresh scent of ammonia was again in the air as she came to the first door on the right. A note card was placed inside a thin copper frame on the large dark brown wooden door:

The Residence of

Ms. Margaret Lynne

Pulling the key that Lena had given her from her pocket, she unlocked the door and dragged herself in. She scanned the room and studied its contents. Each piece of furniture was made of either pine or oak handmade many years ago. Well built, strong and stark. No real distinction or artwork, just basic craftsmanship, like second-rate carpentry. The desk was a roll-top made from maple wood. A stark chair of pine stood in front of it.

The room was simple. She glanced at the small bed with a thin, uneven, tired looking mattress. *It's a fucking cot, an army cot, perhaps from World War One, for God's sake. How the hell do people sleep on these?*

There was a note pinned to the olive drab blanket.

Please excuse the room. We are currently renovating the third floor for you, our guests. New beds are on order and fresh paint is due the second week of September. The bathroom is down the hall. If you are a woman, please disregard the urinals.

Why? They're worried I might try peeing in it? Maggie removed the note, crumpled the paper, and tossed it toward the white plastic basket next to the roll-top desk. It went in.

A twenty-five-dollar co-pay a night for the privilege of sleeping on a hundred-year-old cot. *I'd think they would have paid for themselves before World War II.*

She eased herself down onto the cot. Scenes from a long ago bad dream came to her. She was eight years old again. The shadows and voices returned and the volume ratcheted up a notch. She put her hands over her ears and winced. Seconds later they were gone. She was covered in a cold sweat.

She lay on the cot until calm. Reaching into her bag, she retrieved the pen and journal and shuffled to the desk, opening the journal to begin writing.

August 10, 2001 4:40 PM

What was this place before it was a retreat center, a seminary? I think it was, but my mind is playing tricks on me. I need to call Dr. Fleming...

She entered the experiences at her retreat site starting with the hearse, then Lena, and ended with the voices, shadows, and screams. She added a notation about the furniture: *My brother would have gotten a kick out of seeing my reaction about the urinals and to the army cot.* She put the pen down. Tired, she laid back and fell asleep.

When she woke the room was dark except for the streetlights and glow from the crescent-shaped moon that shown through an open window. She lifted her head off the musty-smelling pillow. Her eyelids were heavy.

She winced as the lump ached and the crusty dried blood on her right eyebrow itched. Tired, sore, and hungry, she yawned and stretched her arms, trying to wake up. In the dim moonlight she stepped to the door and flipped on the light switch.

The room remained dark. She turned toward the desk. There was a lamp sitting next to it on a small end table. She fumbled for the little black light switch below the bulb. The light was dim but manageable.

Sitting back down on the lone sterile chair at the desk, she looked about the room. *Here I sit on an ancient chair in a room with no TV, no computer access; had to leave the cell phone at the front desk with Lena.* She stood and walked to the corner of the room.

On each side of the room was a window. On the left she could see the winding road leading to the front entrance. On the end she looked across a narrow lane that circled the building. A grand red brick two-story Victorian house stood on the other side of the lane. The windows were well lit. It made her think of funeral homes and all the rooms held a body in a casket for viewing. She felt a chill.

Suddenly loud bolts of thunder and thin shards of oblong crystal pierced her sanity. Her eyes widened as they flew right through her eye sockets. And then the voices came. *Shame on you–you little sinner. Take off your clothes! Use the chamber pot at the end of the bed. How much money will we get for her? How much for her brother? You'd better write a good-bye letter to your parents. Put this wig on. Such a pretty, pretty girl.*

The attack brought her to her little girl knees. The visions and whispered words of a man in black came at her fast. The sights and sounds were both deafening and overwhelming. She fell to the floor, covering her ears as she screamed in horror.

Her heart pounded fast and hard, as she lay sprawled on the floor below the window. Curling into a fetal position, she pressed her hands hard against her ears as tears flowed to the hardwood floor. Minutes passed before she regained her composure–and her sanity.

Seated again at the desk, she opened the second bottle of water, and dug into the bag and pulled out her meds. She counted out three tablets each from three bottles, and placed them in groups of three on the desk next to her journal. She had to make another entry.

The pain reached level seven. Doctor Aaron Betz instructed her to take as many as necessary. "Fifteen if you have to."

That would be too many, she thought; in fact, she was sure of that. She didn't want to die by accident. She took nine.

"Timmy. Are you listening?" she said aloud. "I could use a little help here, bro."

***

9:15 PM

Cancer isn't for pussies. Ovarian cancer sucks the bag big time. Lymph node cancer is devious at best. You never know what part of the body will feel the ugly pangs of pain. They're sudden and piercing. It's a distressing with a fatal feeling. Plus, it hurts like hell.

Maggie pulled out half of her sandwich from the small refrigerator in the corner. It was simply peanut butter and strawberry jelly on sourdough from the Hula Java café. A half-pint of milk had been placed in the small refrigerator by Lena. She sat at her desk, opened it, and grabbed a handful of her meds. With two bites of the sandwich and half of the milk, the pills pass beyond the esophagus, down to where the body digests and absorbs the tiny tablets of comfort.

She picked up the pen again.

God, I can't take much more of this. I'd rather die than lose my sanity. One thing at a time, please. I've got enough trouble. Give me a break, Big Guy.

Sanity, where do I find it? No TV, radio, or telephone in the rooms. This place is an island unto itself … far away from reality. The building is seventy, ninety years in the past, at best.

Seventeen pages later she put the pen down. The pain was gone. She didn't get sick.

She pulled off her golf shirt as she thought of her late brother, Timmy Lee. So sad, she thought, that he had died too young. *God, how I miss him.*

She removed her capris and laid them at the foot end of the bed. She breezed over to the side window that faced the redbrick Victorian. All the shades had been pulled and the house stood in darkness. It gave her the creeps.

The evening lights danced off the power lines that stretched from pole to pole. The window, though old and untouched for God knows how long, was not a problem for Maggie. With two light pushes, she had the lower half up as far as it would go, and let the comfort of a rare Midwest August breeze flow around her body.

There she stood, gazing out the window as she removed her size 34-C black Vanity Fair French cut bra and matching panties. She stood naked looking out at the calm serenity of a warm summer's night. She could feel the night's air on her skin as it circled around and through her tummy and legs. It felt sensual, erotic.

It was a peaceful moment as she combed back her thinning hair with her fingers. It was a miracle that she had any hair left after the three sets of chemotherapy.

Her dyed dark brown hair stayed in place along her well-tanned face. Her eyebrows were less than pencil thick resting above her longer than most, yet concise, nose. Her lips were full with a slight natural pout. A few wrinkles were set in place around her almond-shaped eyes and mouth. But they were refined lines and only enhanced her mature beauty. Maggie looked much younger than the fifty-some years she was, but not to her. She was tired, tired of living in pain and confusion, tired of doctors and meds.

In her black suitcase was her orange and yellow plumeria flowered sarong. She slipped it on along with her flip-flops, and grabbed a pack of Old Golds and lighter. She felt like going downstairs and walking out onto the front steps to enjoy the quiet sounds of midnight out on the edge of the city.

Taking a deep breath, she opened the door and paused, saying, "Okay you fucked-up demons. Stay the hell away. I don't want to hear, see, or smell anything frightening as I enter the hallway, especially the damned stairwell. Dear God, if I do have a panic attack, help me keep the sonofabitch at bay for a few hours. Thanks, I'll owe ya."

Light trickled into her room. It shone from the lone light bulb hanging down from the ceiling at the entrance to the washroom. There was another light bulb at the entrance to the staircase but it was burned out.

She closed the door behind her and locked it. She took the key and dropped it into her cleavage. Her ample breasts would protect it there. She padded along the hall toward the staircase door. At the door she paused and stood silent. She neither heard nor saw anything out of the ordinary. *Damn, those pills are working! I'll just open this big ugly-assed door and dance my way to the first floor and that'll be that, right, God?*

Maggie put both hands on the door, gathered her strength, and jerked it open. She stepped as fast as she could down to the first landing and stopped. A light metallic clanging followed behind her, echoing through the stairwell. She stiffened. Looking down to the side of her right foot, she laughed. Maggie bent down and snatched the dropped room key into the palm of her hand. *They used to be ample.*

As she stepped off the last stair, Dr. Richard Fleming entered her mind. He seemed to be in distress. Call it women's intuition, whatever; he appeared to have a hard time breathing. She shook her head and dismissed the thought. *Too cheap to buy a new air conditioner.*

CHAPTER FOUR

11:25 PM - Scottsdale

I t was almost midnight and it was a hundred and nine. The air conditioner had quit running altogether. Better the a.c. than the fridge, which Richard had just stocked with his favorite sliced Italian prime rib, cured ham, and aged Swiss cheese.

The cigars were in the humidor, and a case of Chivas Regal in the back room. His office was his life. The plaques on the wall told his story. Helping his fellow agents with their problems and problem solving was his expertise. The get-togethers with top agents and his exboss and former client, J. Edgar, was worth all the risk-taking. Richard sipped Chivas on the rocks, studying the pictures on the walls.

Alone. Never married, he had no one to go home to anyway, so what the hell. Why go home?

He thumbed through the yellow pages for his reliable repairman. Craig, an agent retired due to gunshot wounds, had said he'd be there fifteen minutes ago. "Damn it! He's a night owl and he's been here many times at this hour sipping scotch with me. He's never late." It gave him an unexpected, uncomfortable feeling. The doctor was sweating and sitting in front of his small tabletop fan.

"In the meantime," he said talking out loud, "I'll call Gordon, again, and see what he's up to, and let him in on Margaret's condition and whereabouts. I've got one more card up my sleeve and I'm going to play it. He won't believe how I set this up." His thoughts gave him a slight smile as he fat-fingered the digits on the too-small phone.

He sat bent over, concentrating when he felt something odd. The air pressure changed. The old former FBI man had his eyes fixed on the too-small keypad, as a noise behind him interrupted his thoughts. Before he could turn, he felt immediate pressure on his forehead. Dr. Richard Fleming couldn't move.

A thin man wearing sunglasses and a black cap with *U.S. Border Agent* emblazoned in yellow lettering stood holding a knife to his chest. Richard tensed up, squeezing hard on the phone. The heavy hand on his forehead kept him still. Pain shot through his neck, just behind his left ear near his jugular vein. He continued pressing the keypad from memory.

"Just a shot of Pancuronium bromide to paralyze your diaphragm and lungs. Recall the voice, old man?"

He couldn't see the visitor behind him, but knew his voice all too well. He'd heard it on all the tapes. A sly and cunning man, intelligent, and an egotistical sexual deviant. It all added up now. Richard knew who the crazy sonofabitch was, albeit too late. He thought, *Damn it!*

"To be on the safe side, I've another shot for you," the voice said in a cold professional tone.

All of Richard's work was coming to an end. To struggle would do no good, he knew, but he had to try. It was what he had been taught. His instincts kicked in, but he was no match for the two professionals. He knew who was behind him with the needles. *I should have reacted to the bastard sooner.* "Not as sharp as I used to be. My fatal mistake," Richard mumbled as a dull pain pinged behind his ear again. Almost immediately his thoughts slowed down. Try as he might to stay awake and break free, he couldn't get his body to move.

He heard the last words from his old nemesis: "You know the routine. The last shot, as always, is potassium chloride. It'll induce cardiac arrest in just a few seconds, my friend."

Richard thought of his old cronies and the camaraderie they had shared: the poker nights, cigars, and scotch with the guys he had once worked with. The hole-in-one ... His thoughts froze in time at the nineteenth hole and his eyelids went to half-mast. Darkness overtook Richard and he saw himself in a long dark tunnel. There was nothing now but blackness. All was quiet. No light, no sounds. Then nothing. The phone remained gripped in his hand.

"Now strangle him with the piano wire. When you're done, put the wire in the hands of the dead man out there on the stairwell. It'll look like an old patient came back for revenge. I'll take his implant."

Kurt added his newfound thrill of leaving his calling card on the dead man. A jab to the neck with his knife blade and the letters, FLOC, sliced into his forehead.

CHAPTER FIVE

12:00 AM CST

Ambling away from the staircase and down the hall she notices a dim light at the front desk. She pauses. There, an elderly man sat at the desk, reading a paperback book from the light of a too small desk lamp. He squints as he leans in toward the light. She steps to the desk as he looks up. His hair is thick, curly, and pepper gray. He's wearing a light tan short sleeve silk shirt with loose fitting wrinkle free brown pants and a black belt. He appears solid and trim. Strong dark hands and long fingers gently hold the book on the table.

He looked up at her and questioned, "Miss Lynne, what in the world are you doin' up at this hour of the night?"

She rested her folded arms on the desk and leaned in, exposing a good portion of her breasts as they spilt over the top of her wrapped sarong. The lily-whites got his attention. "I thought I might sit out on the front steps and take in the night air," she said nodding. "You got my name off the clipboard hanging on the wall there next to the desk, right? Am I the only ... guest here tonight?"

"Yes'um. You the one and only."

"I was afraid of that," she said with a sigh. "Your name?"

"Curtis Miles Presley with a capital P, ma'am."

"Call me Maggie," she said, grinning with pursed lips. She stopped. *Lena said the maintenance man was Gunderson, not Presley.* He didn't look like the hearse driver she saw earlier. She didn't sense any coldness about this man. He felt ... safe. "Care to join me?"

He fastened a paper clip on the page he was reading, closed the Gayle Lynds spy thriller, and pushed back the chair and stood up. "You can call me Curtis. Now, I'm only five foot six and a half, but it's all me, naturally."

The gentleman took her arm as he pushed open one side of the double door entrance. They sat down together on the top step.

"Thank you, Curtis, she said. "And you've been here, how long?"

"Since Jesus was spittin' up and droolin'. Seems like it anyway. I arrived here in 1950 with no money in my pockets. Shortly, they gave me the job of bein' the first colored janitor here. About ten years later they called me a Negro janitor. Then I became a black man in the sixties. Nowadays there ain't no color to me.

"They finally accepted me for who I am, Curtis Miles Presley. Yup, fifty-plus years in one place. Saw many a changes. I ain't but a few months from being eighty years old. Can you believe that? Eighty! Don't feel eighty. There's still a fifteen-year-old kid in me somewhere. I still got a feel for life and an eye for a woman."

Maggie sat with her feet on the second step. She pulled on the fabric of her sarong, and folded it up just above her knees and, placed her forearms there as she leaned to a relaxed position and listened to the old man's story.

She looked over to meet his eyes then glanced away. "So you're saying there *is* a chance for me. You might try to hustle me?"

Curtis saw through her question like a professional therapist. "Yeah, *ma'am*. I might just try and hustle you up. You 'bout the right age for me, young lady. There could be trouble though. I'm still in my prime. I could wear you out!"

For a second there was silence. Maggie lifted her head looking straight ahead and with a slight jolt, began laughing out loud. Curtis joined in. Maggie hadn't laughed so hard in years. Tears rolled down her cheeks. Curtis offered his kerchief.

"Thank you, Curtis, I needed that," she said as she dabbed at the corners of her eyes. She had to ask though, "What's with this place? It seems like an odd place to send me. I mean it looks like it's used for something else, like a monastery or something. You know what I mean?

He shook his head and took a breath, "Let's see, he said glancing about the starlit sky, "It was once a minor seminary for boys but it closed in January of nineteen fifty.

"That's when I come around. In the early summer of that year they hired me. The one they had, a white man, hung hisself around Easter time from that big oak tree there by the front entrance. Now, as back then, the old priests reside in the right wing, naturally."

Maggie smiled and couldn't help interrupting, "Right wing, *naturally?*"

He nodded, "Naturally," and continued with his story in a matter of fact way, up to the present.

"Ain't been but a few stragglers like yourself been through here lately. The last old wrinkly priest died here a few months ago. Ain't been one here, since, neither. In fact you'll be the last patient until all the renovations has been done to the buildin'. They going to stop the program of lettin' folks like you in here. I got it from a *source.*

"A men's group, an all-white men's group from Hawaii, is buyin' the place. That's the rumor, anyway. The Big Island. I suppose when that happens they goin' to give me my release papers, too." At that, his head sank and his eyes watered.

Maggie slid over as her body touched his, and put her arms around her new friend, hugged him and kissed his cheek. She hugged him again as they sat side by side. She put her arms back in her lap as she leaned forward. He just sat there with his hands folded.

"It's a bitch gettin' old, Maggie. The Doc says my ticker's giving out. I ain't told anybody but you."

His frankness caught her off guard. Besides she wanted an answer about Gunderson.

"Curtis, I have to ask you something. Who's Kurt Gunderson and what does he do here?"

Pausing, he squinted as he cleared his throat and spat into the bushes. "That man's trouble. You stay away from him, Miss Lynne. He's been here for a while, off and on. He and I don't talk."

"Lena feels about the same way as you do," Maggie said. "She never told me to stay away from him. Just that he was cranky."

"That's Lena," he said. "Always tryin' to find good in a person. Not to change the subject but, you have a middle name or is it just Maggie Lynne?"

"Curtis Miles," she explained, "my parents named me Magdalene, and I absolutely adored it. As I grew, my school friends and others called me names. It seems the name equates to a whore, or a prostitute. That's what the Bible says about her."

Curtis interrupted, "Mary Magdalene wasn't, you know."

"Wasn't what?" She asked.

"A prostitute," he said with conviction as his head nodded. "She was a special friend of the Master. She loved Jesus. He loved her back. She's the Holy Grail."

She shot him a questioning look. "How would you know?"

"Let it be, Ms. Lynne."

They sat silent on the front steps with their thoughts. Watching together as a huge majestic stag trotted even paced near the front gate. He was in velvet as his antlers shown below a streetlight as he passed by. Graceful. Strong.

"Married?" she asked.

"Oh, I was married to the most wonderful woman in the world. She was tall, thin and could play all kinds of sports. She could run like the wind and swear a blue streak.

"Alisha had a wild and restless side to her, but I settled her down a bit. And when there was just the two of us ... ooh-wee! The best lover I ever had. So tender to the touch, good-natured too, she was.

"She watched other people's children and took in their wash. She couldn't have children. I didn't mind. The good Lord took my Alisha from me back in Eighty-eight. Best woman in the world. I just ain't been the same without her."

"You know Curtis Miles Presley with a capital P, on your way to the pharmacist you'll have to stop by the hardware store and get yourself a wheel barrow."

He sat gazing straight ahead as he asked, "What you talkin' about woman? What pharmacist? Why'd I need a wheelbarrow?"

She said, "If you truly intend to wear me out, darlin', you're going to need a wheelbarrow full of Viagra, kid. You don't know who you're messin' with."

Maggie leaned her forearm on his shoulder as she stood to walk back inside, leaving Curtis by himself. Just before the door closed, she thought she could hear a hushed, "Hee-hee" coming from her new friend and confidante.

Her thoughts of Curtis Miles Presley continued down the hall and up the three flights of steps with out incident, down the hall and to her room.

August 10, 2001 1:15 AM

Tonight I met the nicest man. Curtis Miles Presley with a capital P. An old man, a wise man. He was a friend in need tonight. I needed him and it seemed he needed me. We agreed on many things, including our distrust for the janitor.

Lena has a funny way with words. What I would call a mortuary, she calls a funeral parlor; words from yesteryear. Haven't met the visiting nurse, yet.

She removed the wool blanket from the cot and her sarong. She lay naked on the cot as a welcomed cool breeze drifted through the screens.

Thank you, God. See how you are? She thought about her new friend, bad ticker and all. She also had an opposing thought. A woman doesn't always need a man. She smiled at the thought of her sex toy in the suitcase and eased into a deep sleep.

Later that night she rolled to one side and pushed the little brass button on her leather strapped gold wristwatch. 2:45. She rolled back and with both hands she gently petted and caressed the pubic hair above her vagina before massaging her clitoris.

It's getting long. I'll have to trim that bush tomorrow, it'll feel smooth again and more erotic. It always has.

She drifted off to dreamland while thinking of the simplistic, gentle yet engaging man who sat with her out on the front steps. There was something about the old man. He seemed so alive.

As Maggie drifted, she kept hearing his words, "She wasn't, you know. Mary Magdalene wasn't a prostitute. She loved Jesus. Jesus loved her back."

Miles? Someone had that name a long time ago. Nothing registered.

Mr. Curtis Miles Presley with a capital P. Alisha had herself a good man. Goodnight, my friend. She was tired. For once, she felt no pain.

CHAPTER SIX

August 11 - 7:30 AM

Lena's knuckles were raw from knocking on Maggie's door. She set the tray of scrambled eggs, bacon, hash browns, milk and orange wedges, down on the floor, banged on the door with both hands, and called her name.

She heard a moan. Startled, she turned and spotted Maggie down the hall leaning against the washroom wall. She had the wool blanket draped around her shoulders. She looked like death warmed over as she teetered toward Lena. Her rubbery legs buckled. She collapsed in the hallway, rapping her forehead hard against rock hard marble tile. Blood flowed and kept flowing this time. It formed a large dark red purplish pool around her head and face.

Lena waddled as fast as she could in the opposite direction, heading for the stairway.

***

"Hello ... Anybody home? Are you there, Margaret?"

She heard the man's voice and tried to speak. She forced her eyes open. The room was bright. She squinted.

A man in a white jacket leaned over and said, "Like Humpty-Dumpty, you had a great fall."

A paramedic behind him said, "We'll be on our way then."

Dr. Morris Gallagher from the University hospital nodded in appreciation as they stepped past him and went out the door.

"No rush, but when you feel ready I want to help you sit up, so you can take your medicine. I've been on the phone with Dr. Betz. He doesn't think you've been taking your medication at the proper intervals. It's six tablets of each, every four hours," he nodded.

Her head throbbed and the room was spinning, yet with his help she managed to sit up. When she did, the bedsheet fell from her chin to her lap, exposing her breasts.

Groggy, trying to make sense and be present, she mumbled, "How 'bout these knockers, Doc?" she said as her eyes rolled. "Six? I'm confused." She shook her head.

"I've seen a thousand breasts and I'll see a million more. Yes, six is what he said." He glanced about the room, resting his eyes on Lena who was standing near the far corner of the room. Her blushing face was turned away, no doubt from the patient's inadvertent exposure.

Maggie pulled the sheet up to her chin as the doctor placed the pills in her mouth one at a time and gave her a glass of water. She sipped the water at first and then she tried to gulp the rest as it spilled down the sheet in front of her. It made her cough and some of the water shot through her nostrils dripping onto the floor. She handed the glass back to the doctor and sobbed, "I'm a goddamn mess. My head hurts."

"It should hurt," he said. "I put seven stitches in your scalp just inside your hairline, between your left ear and eyebrow. Lena just brought in some homemade chicken noodle soup in the bowl, on the tray. I want you to sit here and eat it all before I leave. I'm going downstairs to call your doctor. If you need me, have Lena call Chloe, she's my aide, and a damned fine nurse. You'll like her. She knows where to get a hold of me.

"Your crotch?" Maggie mumbled.

Dr. Gallagher sighed, "At least your sense of humor is intact." He turned to leave the room. "Chloe will be in later. She'll be your visiting nurse."

Moments later he was downstairs on the phone with Dr. Betz's secretary. *"What?* How? When did this happen?" Morris listened to the stunning news. He replaced the receiver back on the hook as he regained his composure. *Perhaps I should say nothing. In a month at most, it won't matter anyway.*

***

"I'm so embarrassed, Lena." Her mind was swimming from the pills. Her eyes reddened.

"Now, now," Lena said as she stepped to her side. "Don't you worry about a thing, Ms. Lynne. I'll clean up here and help you as much as you like. Just put your laundry outside the door whenever you want. Anything at all, just call on me. We're moving you to the first floor tomorrow. I won't miss the hike to the third floor, though Lord knows I could lose a little weight here and there," she puffed.

"I hate being sick and needy, Lena, and that reoccurring *dream.* I see silent death screams, like the scream of an unborn baby when the needle pierces through the womb.

"That silent scream, I hate it! I can't shake it. But it's not a baby I hear. It's someone else. Sorry. I don't mean to rant and rave."

Tears rolled down her cheeks as she tugged on Lena's hand, and pulled her to the cot. Lena perched herself next to Maggie. They sat and had a good cry together. The cot moaned and creaked but didn't collapse.

Maggie blew her nose and said, "Some advice, kid. Don't get cancer."

Lena nodded solemnly. "Just so you know, I put a chamber pot at the foot end of the bed for you. Just use the porcelain if you're feeling dizzy or sick. It's all right by me. I don't want to see you fall down by the washroom again. You scared the bejesus out of me."

Lena pushed hard off the cot. She clomped to the open doorway, dabbing a Kleenex to her eyes. Then she turned, laboring up the hall to the stairwell.

What was left of Wednesday, August eleventh, Maggie spent examining the latest bump on the head, sleeping and slurping chicken noodle soup, and later, a cup of beef broth. She munched on Saltines while journaling, until she heard the call of nature. Recalling Lena's admonition to use the chamber pot, she frowned.

I've used slits in the ground, but to hell with the pot. I'd hate like hell to die on it and have somebody discover my slumping body sitting on that damn thing. Some stupid bastard at the coroner's office would have the picture plastered all over the goddamned Internet.

She maneuvered it with her feet, as she sat on the cot and put her heels to the front of it, and gave the ornately painted porcelain chamber pot a push. It slid on the hardwood floor under the cot, towards the wall. She shuffled down the hall to the washroom and back.

Every four hours she took her medication, three tablets each, not six as the doctor had ordered. Just before dozing off at 1:00 AM, she said a small prayer: "God, if you're busy just send an angel of healing or mercy. I could use one now. Thanks, I'll owe you another, Amen."

CHAPTER SEVEN

4:30 AM August 12

S he used the tissue carefully, flushing the urinal, and after chucking the tissue in one of the toilets, she flushed that as well.

"I did it. I peed in a urinal! First time for everything, huh, Missy?" she said to the mirror. "Shower time! Better get the power saw and trimming gear and mow that forest down there."

She placed her Lady Remington and her bag of toiletries on the stainless steel shelf that ran above the length of the washbasins. The bag contained an array of her essentials including: toothbrush and paste, eyeliner, a two ounce bottle of Royal Hawaiian Wicked Wahine cologne mist, an ounce bottle of L'Air du Temps mist, a small jar of vitamin E moisturizing cream, a tube of Wild Honeysuckle body lotion, Secret deodorant, and a little plastic bottle of Dew Drops personal lubricant.

She stood in front of the mirror as she dabbed off the shower water with the small, over-used white towel, next to the first washbasin with the hand towel and washcloth.

She stepped close to the mirror while examining the stitches just inside her hairline. *I'll be damned, no swelling.* She touched the stiff texture of the black thread. *Christ, it doesn't even hurt! My eyebrow isn't puffy, either.*

Maggie felt a tingling sensation that began in the palms of her hands and spread throughout her body. It was a feeling of excitement. She was thinking of Curtis Miles as a strong young man.

For the first time in a long time, she was feeling aroused early in the morning. Late at night–in bed, dreamy-eyed–didn't count. She was giddy now and snapped her legs together, then relaxed with her feet shoulder-length apart.

Maggie stepped back and looked at her image in the mirror again, dropping the towel to the floor. She eyed herself from head to toe and back again. She realized the power she had been missing, that awesome power of her womanhood.

All right, girl, let's clear that thick, black forest. She eyed herself in the mirror, reached for the Skintimate aromatherapy moisturizing shaving gel, razor, and the warm wet washcloth. She loved the feel of bare, smooth skin around her inner thighs and her vagina. Standing back, she admired herself in the mirror.

Erotic, sexual images entered her seductive brain cells as she thought of using the dewdrops. Glancing at her watch, she thought of Lena plodding up the steps with her breakfast. *Oh, hell, it's only five-o-five.* She stepped close to the mirror and saw her breath on it as she exhaled.

With the plastic bottle in hand she flipped the lid and placed several drops on her right index finger and set the plastic bottle on the stainless steel ledge. Tilting her head back, she closed her eyes.

She climaxed. Twice. The mirror fogged over.

***

Back in her room Maggie set the pen down next to her journal. She flipped it shut and placed it in the white burlap bag. The envelope of prescriptions and instructions lay at the bottom of the bag. She was instructed to follow it "to a T," as per Dr. Fleming's orders. AA meetings. Hmm.

***

"Ahem, good morning, Ms. Lynne. Your breakfast is here. You look *so* much better today!" Lena walked through the propped-open door and set the food tray on the cot.

"Thank you, Lena. I feel a hundred percent better. But please, call me Maggie." Looking down at her list of instructions, she asked, "Lena, I have to get to an AA meeting. Is there one around here?"

Lena snapped her fingers and said, "You know what, old Kurt Gunderson's been out of town the last couple of days, but I'll see if he's back. I'll give the old fart a call. Be right back."

"Oh, Lena," Maggie shouted after her as she was already at the steps, "The second meeting of the day is at eight o' clock." There was no response.

Shrugging, she took her prescribed medication, three pills at a time. Stepping over to the small closet next to the cot, she looked over the clothes she had brought along.

She slipped on the eggshell white sleeveless silk blouse she had purchased at the Ala Moana shopping mall near Waikiki Beach months earlier. Her black pedal pushers seemed inviting. She grabbed them off the hanger and padded to the washroom clad only in her peach-colored French-cut panties. She loved the feeling of free boobs.

At the mirror she pulled on her pedal pushers and zipped up. Reaching for the silk blouse, she put her arms through it and stood looking in the mirror. Her nipples became perky against the smooth silk blouse. *They're happy.* She laughed.

The pain eased to level three as Maggie walked barefoot back down the hallway feeling the best she had felt in a week. She slipped on a pair of Alpargata sandals she bought while digging for bones in Guatemala years ago. She stepped out of her room with her wallet in her bag, along with a Callaway golf cap, and took a few steps up the pale green hallway to the staircase.

She adjusted the bag over her left shoulder and placed both hands on the doorknob. As she did, she got the shivers. The old door seemed heavy. She tugged and pulled. The doorknob turned as the heavy old door begrudgingly obliged.

The wind began making a whooshing sound because of the draft of the warm air rising and forcing its way through the crevasses of the doorway.

All at once it gave way, and the door pushed itself open as she let go. The force pushed her backward. Maggie regained her footing and started down the steps.

Just as she reached the first landing the door slammed shut with a loud, heavy crashing sound. It shook the stairwell as the noise echoed. Maggie screamed as she made contact with both feet on the landing, and leaned against the far wall. She turned, looking up at the door as the voices returned.

It was different this time, just one voice. *Return to the chamber pot. The writing is on the wall.* The echoes became louder. *He knows. Go to him. He knows, downstairs.* And just like that, it stopped.

Blood pounded in her throat as she caught her breath. Her skin grew clammy as she continued down the shadowy stairway to the landing between the first and second floors. The stairway narrowed. It began twisting and turning. She held onto the railing as her pulse pounded in her ears. Her palms were sweaty.

She nearly panicked, but managed to keep her cool and turn her fear into power.

"Listen, whoever you are, *whatever* you are that's scaring me." Her voice was strong. "I am *female*. I am Woman! Go away before I set your balls on fire, you *bastard!*" Not waiting for a reply, she flew down the steps.

When she set foot on the first floor, she stopped and pulled out the Callaway cap. She set down the bag and pulled back her hair, put the cap on and pulled her hair through the gap above the Velcro strip.

Still breathing hard, she pulled the bag onto her left shoulder, turned, and walked down the hallway to the desk. Halfway up the hall Lena was half running, half walking toward her.

"What's wrong, Ms. Lynne? What happened? Are you all right?" She asked.

"Oh, Lena. Did you hear the voices?" she asked in between breaths.

"Just yours, Ms. Lynne. Kurt said for you to find your own way to the meeting. I'm going to the laundry room now, and get your room ready here on the first floor. Chloe will be here later. She's got a good heart."

Maggie looked past Lena as a figure walked through the front door. It was a man wearing a straw hat. He stopped, doffed his straw hat, waving it in her direction. Maggie raised a hand and waved back.

"Oh, Maggie, you and I have to have a chat." Lena rubbed her hands together as she spoke.

"Sorry, maybe later, Lena. I have a meeting to attend."

"As you wish," Lena replied as she tramped the other way stopping and turning toward the hallway heading south, and glancing back.

Maggie breezed straight ahead to the front desk where the gentleman stood, resting himself on the counter. "Good mornin' pretty woman. It's goin' to be a hot one t'day."

"Morning, Curtis."

Lena peeked around the corner in Maggie's direction saying, "Are you sure you're up to the task?"

Looking back to Lena, she paused and said, "I'll be all right. I got a lot of sleep yesterday and last night.

Curtis said, "Ain't nothin' goin' to happen to nobody as long as I'm around." He stood erect and put his hat back on, tapped it in place as he took Maggie's arm. They passed through the double doors. Standing outside on the top step, Curtis looked straight ahead as he spoke.

"Maggie, are you all right?" he asked. "You look like you seen a ghost."

Just a voice in my head and the goblins in the stairwell, she thought. But she tried to make light of his remark. "Funny you should say that. I used to talk to one now and again, but that was years ago."

Curtis's eyes widened. "Well, just the same, it's okay with me if you say you saw a ghost around here. It happens. Like I said the other night, I've been here fifty-plus years and I heard all kinds of ghost stories. People used to say this place is haunted."

Maggie's eyes narrowed with suspicion. *Oh, peachy! My doctor sends me to a haunted house for recovery.*

The old light green auto parked just to the right of the front entrance caught her eye. "Is that—your car?"

Curtis Miles took her arm as they walked down the steps. He opened the passenger door placing his hand on her elbow; he said with a voice of pride, "She's a 1953 Chevy Biscayne. She's got a three-speed-on-the-column so anybody could learn to shift it. I bought it on credit the summer of '57 for my Alisha. Still purrs like a kitten." He shut the door, and walked around and slid into the drivers seat. "Ain't no seat belts to worry about in this jalopy."

"Love it! Can't wait to ride in it with the windows rolled down," she said.

Curtis beamed, "That's good, 'cause she don't have any air conditioning."

He turned the key and pressed the chrome button on the front panel. The engine turned over. He pressed the clutch, shifted the stick on the steering column down to first gear, and then eased out the clutch as they made their way up past the oak tree, and out the front gate.

He turned right onto the two-lane street and said without taking his eyes off the road, "I spent some time at these meetin's you're goin' to. Years ago I drank trying to get along without my Alisha. Got straight and no longer get the blues like I used to."

"You're a sweetheart," she replied. "Will you be at the Evergreens tonight? Thought we could sit outside again and chat."

Curtis smiled and said with a laugh, "I'll be there with bells on my toes."

She smiled then turned back to look at the Evergreens with apprehension. "Good," she said. "I've got a lot to talk about. A lot of questions, I mean."

Smiling, he drove on. Neither said a word until he got near their destination.

"It's that little red brick converted schoolhouse there, under the big oak on the right." As she got out of the car Curtis called out to her,

"You stay put until I come back. The doctor wants to give me some kind of radioactive heart test this morning. Should be back when you get done. I'm serious, now. You stay here 'til you see this little green Chevy comin' up the drive, you hear?"

"Yes sir," she said, saluting him. "I hear you loud and clear. Now hear this!" With a conspiratorial smile she said, "You tell that doctor of yours to go easy on you. I don't want to have to wear you out tonight."

"Yes ma'am," he said with a sharp salute as he drove off.

She thought she could hear a faint, 'hee-hee' coming from his direction. She giggled.

***

Maggie turned toward the entrance to the little redbrick school building. There were picnic tables on the grass on both sides of the paved walk to the front door. On the right stood a man and woman talking to a woman seated at a picnic table, smoking a cigarette. She had her legs crossed and dangled a brown penny loafer at the end of her toe.

Like the building, the table had seen its better days. The large old oak tree that graced the front of the building was in full leaf. It gave plenty of much-needed shade for those coming, going, or just hanging out. Maggie guessed it must have been over a hundred years old. *If it could talk, such stories it could tell.*

CHAPTER EIGHT

7:50 AM

Two middle-aged men near the left front corner of the building stood smoking and talking. They looked in her direction. One nodded. She smiled; they smiled. She pressed her lips together, remembering that she forgot to put on lipstick.

She stepped quicker toward the steps. *First things first,* she said to herself as she went off to find the ladies room.

As she sat on the commode, she thought of her daughter. *Why won't she at least call? Wouldn't do any good,* she realized; *I turned my phone in to Lena. I'll check it when I get back–maybe the email at the Hula Java café. Curtis' lunch will be on me.*

She came out of the ladies room looking like a lady should, with fresh lipstick and eyeliner. One would have to look hard to see the stitches. She arranged her hair and Callaway cap so that it would be nearly impossible for anyone to notice.

Glancing at her watch, she saw it was five minutes to eight. No one was seated. She took her place in one of the many chairs in the last row against the wall, and sat down. She set the bag down on the seat on her right and pulled out her journal. Inhale exhale. Inhale exhale. Inhale exhale. Margaret did her deep breathing exercises until she felt calmer and in a meditative state of mind.

There *was* a moment of serenity. It eased her mind enough to say a prayer for her daughter:

God forgive me my sins. Allow me to be the mother Bliss wants me to be. Keep me strong and spiritually connected to my Higher Power at all times. I call upon your highest angels to protect my daughter and keep her safe. I ask nothing for myself, but to be pain-free until my death. So it is, and thanks for listening, Amen. P.S., What the hell is going on at The Meadows, regarding the crazy stairwell?

The meeting room filled with others, one and two at a time, until there were twenty-seven men and women of all ages, colors, and various walks of life. The room buzzed with quiet chatter. The two chairs on her left remained unoccupied.

At five minutes past the hour, a gray-haired woman about Maggie's age stepped to the podium and took the mike out of its stand. It squealed throughout the room. The thumping of her finger on the mike amplified the squealing, to everyone's displeasure.

"Ahem. My name is Randeinne," she said, leaning to one side of the podium. "I want to welcome everyone to the eight o' clock Capital City AA meeting."

Everyone in the room chimed in, "Good morning, Randeinne." She gave a quick obligatory smile to those in attendance and continued.

"As you know, this is a special meeting as announced for the past several weeks. We have a guest speaker with us this morning. He's an inspirational speaker, former police officer, and a longtime friend of Bill W. He'll be sharing this morning and also tomorrow night at the 10:00 PM meeting. His wonderful wife, who has been an Al-Anon member for, ah, many years, will accompany our guest and speak to Al-Anon members as well.

"This morning, let's start the meeting with our traditional Serenity prayer. It'll be followed by the reciting of the Twelve Steps and Traditions."

She led as the group joined in with, *"God, grant me the serenity to accept the things I cannot change ... "*

Margaret joined in. She was comfortable sitting alone in the back row. The others stood together holding hands. She didn't feel the need to hold hands with strangers. Not today.

As they prayed, her mind forced her back in time.

Raymond Polanski was a third-shift central office technician at the phone company. They met during a tailgating party. It was mid-October. The college football game preceded the Homecoming dance and weekend parties. He was tall, blond, and boyishly handsome. He was also arrogant, bisexual, and a terrific liar.

While working for the telephone company, he farmed the land his father had left him. He couldn't repair a tractor or plow a straight line. Needless to say, Ray was a lousy farmer.

He married Maggie to please his mother *and* to stay in the closet. His father left the picture soon after his birth. Raymond did everything to please his demanding perfectionist of a mother. She didn't know he swung both ways.

He couldn't tell her that he had an ongoing relationship with his mentor, Lawrence Burke, who had taught him about sex between a priest and altar boy. Everything.

He married Maggie when she was a naive twenty-year-old college senior majoring in Archaeology. Curiosity of ancient societies and digging up ancient artifacts became her passion. Finding the remains of people, who had dreams and passions just like herself, was something she enjoyed. It had also caused her to seek a therapist when she was a sophomore.

"... the courage to change the things I can, and the wisdom to know the difference." The group raised their hands above their heads and chimed, "Keep coming back. It works!" They released hands, and sat down.

"The Twelve Steps, as it is done in AA," she continued. The attendees echoed the words they read off the black and white posters on the smoke-stained walls, *"One. We admitted we were powerless over alcohol-that our lives had become unmanageable."*

An older couple appeared at the doorway near Maggie. They stepped in. She could smell the fragrance of Chanel No. 5.

She glanced up from underneath the bill of her cap. The newcomers smiled her way and sat down after reciting Step One along with the others.

A bolt and flash sent Maggie reeling. As quick as it came, the sudden jarring left. Looking at the couple again, she realized they were still looking her way. Rather than acknowledging them, she dropped her head, staring at the floor. Her palms became clammy. The lady sitting next to her seemed somehow familiar. So, too, was the man she was with.

A soft angelic voice entered Maggie's head:

"My dear Margaret Lynne, Step Two is coming. Are you prepared? Can you now surrender your thoughts and listen to your Higher Power?"

Oh, no. Not now, she thought as she grabbed her pen and journal from her handbag. She wrote the words that entered her mind.

"Step Two," the group continued, *"Came to believe a power greater than ourselves could restore us to sanity."*

The Voice was back, saying, "Return to the chamber pot, the writing is on the wall. He knows downstairs, he knows...." She set the pen down and looked up and away from her journal. *Again this morning, I heard voices,* she thought. "What does it mean?" she breathed out loud.

Maggie blushed, mumbling, "Forgive me, I was thinking out loud." She collected her things into her bag and excused herself as she began stepping past the two, leaving the roomful of chanting recovering alcoholics and their significant others.

Walking outside of the building to the shaded picnic table out front, she removed her cap and let her hair down. She felt faint. Resting her head on her folded arms atop the cool wooden table, she breathed easier.

After a few moments she raised her head only to discover the lady who had sat next to her followed her out.

"Are you all right?" she asked.

"Better now, thank you." Regaining her composure, Maggie combed back her thinning hair with her fingers. "I don't know what I was thinking in there. If I bothered you, please–"

"No, not at all," she said. "I was just a little worried. You looked a bit ... pale. I came out to see how you were doing. I'm glad to see your color is back. You look much better."

"Thanks. I'm Maggie, by the way."

"My name is Kathryn, Kathryn Maxwell. Call me Kat."

Reaching for her hand, Maggie's response was calm and cool as goose bumps covered her skin.

"I'm Margaret Lynne. Please, have a seat." Kat sat across from her at the table. "Your voice sounds somewhat familiar, but I can't place it," Maggie said as she massaged her temples.

Smiling, Kathryn said, "Now, that's interesting. I once knew a young girl named Margaret Lynne. She lived about an hour from here, out in the country. Her last name was Hornsby. Margaret Lynne Hornsby. The last time I saw her, she wasn't yet ten years old. That was back, oh God, I don't even want to say.

"Anyway," Kathryn went on, "I roomed at her house for a little more than a year, while I taught at the Penn Hollow one-room school-house. It was near a quaint little village called Pine Nut. Margaret was one of my pupils."

"Oh, God forbid there'd be two of us," Maggie groaned, trying to hide her emotions.

Kathryn put her caring hand on Maggie's shoulder as she stood to go back inside, "Are you coming back inside? I'll walk with you."

She's daffy. I'm getting dizzy again.

A light green car came rumbling up the road. It looked like Curtis at the wheel. Maggie rose from the table, teetering and looking his way. She pulled her bag onto her shoulder.

"Come. I invite you to listen to my husband's talk."

Another flash of light shot through Maggie's eyes. A vision of a younger Kathryn stood in the back yard, pushing Maggie's little brother on the new swing set.

She was not going back inside, not with her. Curtis was her ticket out.

"Damn. You know what?" Maggie said, taking a deep breath. Faking the theatrics, she feigned disappointment as she said, "My ... my ride came early. I'll try to make it tomorrow, though." Maggie started for Curtis's car as he leaned from the steering wheel and opened the pas-senger door for her.

Kat raised her hand as she paced behind Maggie. "And she had a brother, she called after her, almost shouting. "Margaret Lynn Hornsby had a little brother named Timmy. Her father liked rhubarb pies. Christmastime 1949?"

Maggie melted into the car. Closing the door she turned and responded to Kat, "Sorry. I'd have known them had they lived near me." She turned, staring straight ahead, not saying another word as Curtis turned the wheel and drove out onto the road toward Evergreen.

He glanced over. She held her fingertips together in a praying manner. It didn't help.

"You're shakin', girl. You scare me!"

"Oh, Miles. I'm so glad you came along when you did. I met a woman back there who says she knows me. But I don't know her! She said she knew my father *and* my brother."

"Well, what'd she say to you, girl?"

"She said she lived at our house and that she was my teacher! Could I have forgotten a childhood Christmas, Curtis? How could I *not* remember such a thing? How can that *be?*" Maggie put her shaking hands to her face.

The Chevy turned up to the front door of Evergreen Meadows and stopped. Maggie blew her nose and put her handkerchief back into her burlap bag. "Tonight? Out on the steps around midnight?"

Curtis nodded. "I'll be there." Maggie leaned and hugged him for a long moment before getting out of the car.

"You get some rest, girl. You're all trembly."

She waved to him as he drove past the grounds and to the gate. As the pale green 1953 Chevy turned left and glided out and onto the road in front of Evergreen Meadows, it seemed to fade and disappear from view.

The Voice returned: *"Write it down. Write it all down!"*

One thing was for sure, something very strange was happening. She wondered, *Do I call my shrink?* But she quickly dismissed the idea. Doctor Fleming would only sit back and roll his big-assed cigar around in his mouth and say, "Ha! I *told* you."

Sitting on the top step, she reviewed the morning's events. It played out before her like an old black and white movie. The ending was the same as always: she panicked and ran away. From what, though? And from whom? Shaking the hair out of her eyes, Maggie noticed lavender and white flowers in full bloom on both sides of the concrete steps.

The mums were standing tall and thick next to the red-bricked building in loose, rich black soil.

She breathed in the scent once, and then again. Her stomach didn't feel right. She pushed up from the steps and turned to walk back inside and up to her room. *Smells like a funeral parlor to me.*

CHAPTER NINE

9:37 AM

L ena was at the lobby desk when Maggie stumbled in. "I didn't expect you back so soon."

"I don't feel at all well, Lena," Her words slurred as she stopped and stood gazing toward the end of the hallway. It was moving, bending shape, narrowing and widening.

The four-foot-nine Lena waddled out from behind the desk to the hall, grabbing Maggie as her legs buckled.

"You sit on the visitor's chair here, next to my desk."

She helped Evergreen's special guest into the straight-backed upholstered chair.

Maggie thought she was lifted and pulled to a chair years ago within these *very walls* that surrounded her, now.

Her heart pounded at a hard and furious pace. The hallway lights grew dim, her eyes rolled. She blacked out again. Lena was quickly on the phone. "She needs you, Chloe."

The Voice whispered, *"Your mission is not yet complete, Mary Magdalene. There is one more person for you to meet. Face her and all will become clear.*

When Maggie awoke she was lying on a bed in a room off the main corridor. Lena once again was leaning over, perspiring as she fanned her with a rolled-up newspaper.

Maggie's eyes began to flutter as she stirred, moving her head from side to side. All of a sudden she bolted upright, shouting, "Face *who?* And *what* becomes clear?"

Lena all but jumped out of her pantyhose. She dropped the newspaper in her hand and staggered backward, slamming against the brick wall. It kept her from falling to the floor.

"Live or die, girl. Make up your mind," Lena gasped as she plodded down the hallway, shaking off the incident.

***

It's been a hell of a day. It isn't even 11:00 AM, yet I feel a lifetime has passed by me today. Voices, strangers who seem to know me, visions of my past ... what else is there? I have this bitchin' feeling that there's more to come. O Mother Mary, give me strength.

Maggie lay the pen down, took her meds, and slipped out of her dress and underwear. She lay her creamy white nakedness on the fresh cool sheets on a real bed, in the stark, windowless room on the first floor. Her eyelids grew heavy.

It was pitch black when she awoke hours later. Having the urge to pee, she donned her satin robe and found her way down the hallway to a heavy polished oak door. She could just make out the rectangular brass sign at eye-level: WOMEN. Pulling hard on the doorknob, she felt the inner wall to her right for the light switch, flipping it up.

She sat on the white porcelain with a cold wooden seat. Her mind rambled. *Okay boys, what's next? Who's doing the talking? Where are the voices coming from and when will I know what it's all about?*

She flushed and stepped out from the stall and placed the robe on a hook next to the sink and washed her hands and face. She stood in front of the mirror, once again looking at her reflection.

It's not easy to stand naked and face yourself. Look at you, Margaret Lynne. This is you now. Who were you back then, back when you were eight–when you were nine and ten? I was a child my parents loved, that's who, dummy! I looked after my younger brother. I was responsible for him when my parents weren't around. They told me so. It was my duty to protect him. I did my job, did I not?

In the corner of the mirror something strange happened. It began to change color. A hint of yellow glowed, and then brightened. The Voice spoke, *"It wasn't your fault, Mary Magdalene. All is well."*

"All is well, my ass! I'm hearing voices," she answered back. "I've got cancer. It's in the final stages. I'm confused, alone, naked, frightened and dying. *All is well?* Somebody around here is *fucked up!*"

Tears flowed as she grabbed a handful of toilet tissue from the stall and daubed her eyes. She continued. "God, Is this how it's going to be? Am I going crazy in the end? Is this how I die? I need to know, God."

"No, you are not crazy. This is real, as real as Curtis Miles Presley and his 1953 light green Chevy with a three-speed on the column."

The splash of yellow dimmed and disappeared. Her heart pounding, Maggie asked herself, "Now what? I ask a question and the answer is automatic. *From who?*

She found herself journaling when she looked at the time and blurted, "Curtis! Shit."

She felt her way back down the dark hallway to her room, and found her watch. 12:20 AM. "Damn it!" Angry at herself, she tightened the sash around her silk robe, slid her feet into her gold flip-flops, and marched down the hallway to the front steps.

Something else bothered her. Why did she get an image of the lady she and her brother had met when they were kids? And why did the Voice mention Curtis' name? Something was brewing, she was certain of it.

CHAPTER TEN

August 13 12:22 AM

O ut on the edge of Capital City just off of University Avenue, Kathryn Maxwell sat in a quaint old hotel room with her husband, Gordon. She had questions.

"Okay," Gordon answered, "for the sake of argument, suppose it *is* her, and you're sure of it, but she really *doesn't* remember you. What then? They say it's best to let old dogs lie. Trauma will do that to a person. After all, I'd forgotten some of my past, like my freshman year at that minor seminary. Should we try to locate her tomorrow?"

"Maybe ... I don't know. She felt awfully uncomfortable around me," Kathryn said. "As I said before, she got up from the picnic table and said that her ride had come early. She opened the door of the parked car out in front and waved good-bye to me. There was no one in the driver's seat, Gordon, and she didn't *go* anywhere. She just sat there talking to herself and cried. I couldn't watch it any more. I went back inside. I feel bad for her, I really do."

"Well, look," he said with a sigh, "It could be that maybe she's blocked out that part of her life, like a survival technique."

"She saw you too, Gordon. I think she did, anyway," Kathryn answered. "What if she *can* remember you and what you did on that cold winter's night when you picked her up and–"

"You're right," he said, interrupting. "Perhaps it's best that we don't have any further contact with her."

"Gordon," Kat said with a sly grin, "what if you put on your Santa suit and have her sit on your lap again? Like you did when you were the sheriff of Pine Nut?"

"Wrong! What if she comes unglued, and runs in and out of the Serenity House ranting about being tied up and sexually assaulted by Santa Claus or something. Then what, Kat? I'd be screwed. Lord knows we're only here because Richard asked us to be here."

Gordon couldn't help but picture the little eight-year-old girl on that long-ago, cold wintry night. There she was, tied to a chair with duct tape covering her mouth. She looked like a teenager wearing lipstick and a skimpy red dress, her brown hair looked radiant. Margaret was so young yet so traumatized.

He could see himself looking at her, longing to ease her pain. Yet he himself was in pain. He couldn't help himself. He had to touch her, hold her, pick her up and take her away from the others; a place that only he and she knew, a place of sanctuary for the two of them.

He could still feel her tight grip on him as he held her close. Her heart pounded as he held little Margaret, her innocence lost. It was over in a flash. He had to get out and leave her where she was, before he was seen.

"Kat, I think ol' Richard knew she'd be here. I have a gut feeling. I'll call him, first thing in the morning. It may clear up some things."

Kat got the shivers up and down her spine. "Why do I feel uneasy about all of this?"

Gordon shook his head. "I know what you mean. By the way, I got a message just before my speech a few hours ago. I had the phone turned off the last couple of days and didn't know it, so actually I turned it on when I thought I had turned it off. You know, I think there's two messages, texts or whatever the hell you call 'em. Would you be a dear and check it for me? It's humid, I'm hot, and it's late. I'm going to bed."

She fiddled with the phone, finding the place to read text messages, and thumbed the appropriate buttons. "Hey. I don't understand this message. It's about Margaret. I was right! It was her. Gordon, read it! She may be in danger."

She walked the cell to him as he sat on the edge of the hotel bed, one leg out of his shorts, and showed it to him.

"Shhee-it! Keep reading, Kat, I don't have my bifocals."

"The first text is from Richard. If I can decipher this, I think it translates to our friend, Maggie. She's here."

"Aha!"

"You need to see her. He's finished with her sessions, he says. He goes on ... wants you to talk with her about M.G. and Doc? I don't get it. That's all it says.

"Ah, there's another one from him. This one was sent a few hours later on the same day." She read it out loud, stumbling over the abbreviated text-ese and bewildering gibberish that ended the message:

Grdon, ol man, spking at CC Srenty hse? Rembr the semnry—my cli-nt Maggie—shes ther-chek on her-got-bad-vibs-help-its doc- kkkkkkkklg bbbts kkkkkkkklgm

"What the hell is with all the K's?" Gordon asked.

"I have to call Mickey, he said with a sigh. "He may be able to explain M.G. and the doctor bit, I'm guessing, and–well, you know the Mick. He'll have it figured out before I call Aaron. He's got a way of finding out shit you'd never think of, and fast. I'll call him first thing in the morning. I'll be up early."

"And so will I. My stomach is churning."

CHAPTER ELEVEN

12:29 AM

"Hey. Hey, here comes my gal! You look a little better tonight than when I brought you back this morning. You were a wreck."

Breathing heavily, she braced herself on his right shoulder as she stepped down on the first step and then eased herself onto the concrete, and placed her Old Golds next to her. She wanted to speak but didn't know where to begin. Something came over her and it felt good.

She took in the night sights, sounds and smells alongside her new friend. An occasional car passed on the two-lane out front, as they listened to the constant hum of the autos and trucks cruising along the four-lane skirting around the city.

The stars were bright and sparkling in the cloudless upper Midwestern sky. A blinking red light was visible from a high-flying jet; it seemed to meld with the stars and the sounds of the highway.

Maggie suddenly remembered that she forgot. "Curtis Miles, You came back to the Serenity House so soon! You had to take a stress test and all, right?"

Reaching into his front shirt pocket, he pulled out a pack of gum. "A Juicy Fruit for my lady?"

She held the stick of foil-wrapped gum to her nose, remembering the innocent smell. "I haven't had a Juicy Fruit since I was knee-high to a grasshopper," she whispered.

Maggie unwrapped the foil and folded the gum over before placing it in her mouth. She could feel her saliva rushing in to greet the stick of gum. She missed the taste, smell, and excitement of the simple, pleasurable feeling of a time gone by. Then Curtis spoke.

"My doctor called me into his office. He had the heart specialist with him. He did an ultrasound on me and had X-rays taken of my heart a few weeks back. He knows my blood pressure and all of that. Well, the X-rays and ultrasound this morning didn't match what they saw last year.

"They talked. I listened. I talked and they listened. We came to the same conclusion."

Maggie swallowed hard, and down her throat with the saliva went her Juicy Fruit. She coughed a little. Rubbing her nose with her sleeve, she began, "Oh, Curtis, I'm so sorry."

"It's okay, Maggie. I'm not upset. Ain't even angry. It's been comin' for a while, so don't fret for me."

"What'd the doctors say?" she asked with a sigh, putting an arm around his slouched shoulders.

"They begun to talk at once," he said, "then the heart specialist said that he'd done all he could and to do any more ... well, there wasn't much they could do on account of the weakened condition of my heart.

"It won't take any more. It's too weak for any trauma like surgery. A pacemaker won't help either. I got a prescription for some pills, and I don't even know what they're for exactly, but I'm to take them when I feel fluttery or excited."

"How much time?" she asked. Maggie tried to hold in her emotions. "Did they say anything about that?"

He put his arm around her, one sick human being feeling sorry for the other.

"They told me to take things slow. It could be weeks, it could be months. Could happen tomorrow. When I feel tired, I'm to rest. Ain't supposed to be on my feet long and I'm not to get excited." He chuckled a bit, thinking about being *excited.*

"If you were to wear me out–"

Maggie abruptly excused herself and headed inside, saying she'd be right back out.

In the darkness of her room she sifted through her things in her suitcase and underneath her toy of pleasure, she felt the Ziploc bag she was looking for. She headed back down the hallway thinking of Dr. Lois, MD, the name her patients preferred. She had her own methods of madness, and ideas of pharmaceuticals to help patients ease their pain. "Mary" was one of them.

The freckled doctor, Lois, was thought of as the perennial child of the sixties. Her streaked bottle-blonde hair had two foot-long pigtails with purple paisley bows tied unevenly on each one.

Curtis looked relaxed with his arms back, resting his elbows on the concrete as he stretched his skinny legs out in front of him. She sat down next to him again and pulled open the Ziploc bag.

"Whatcha got in there?" he asked.

"Mary J. I'm sure you've seen her, before," she said.

"Are you kiddin' me?" he exclaimed. "If Alisha ever knew of the times I smoked that stuff, she'd kick my butt up around my shoulders!"

They laughed as Maggie pulled out two joints and lit his first, then hers. After several deep inhales and long, shallow exhales, they leaned back again, saying nothing, just gazing at the stars.

"Maggie, I ain't afraid of dyin'. Just so you know. I've come to terms with my situation. The Lord and me had many a conversation, and I'm at peace with myself. So don't you go feelin' sorry for me, 'cause there ain't any need for it. This whole journey just takes me one step closer to my Alisha. You hear me, girl?"

"Aye, aye, Captain," she said with a salute. "That goes for me too, should I go first. I ain't got long, either. Just so you know."

"By the way, this morning when I picked you up, you was all shook up, you called me Miles. Did you know that?"

The nausea had passed and Maggie felt much better. She eased into a mellow fog, hearing everything–though not responding.

"Hey, lady, did you hear me?"

Feeling like she weighed a ton, it was hard to move.

"Yes, Curtis Miles Presley with a capital P., I did call you Miles this morning. The fact is, I wanted out of there so bad that I envisioned you coming up the drive." She stopped a moment, shaking her head at the recollection. "I jumped in the front seat, said something to the lady I was trying to get away from, and suddenly realized I was in somebody else's car. Alone! She went back inside and then you came. I was a mess."

He toked on his joint again, taking a long drag, and lay back again before exhaling.

He sat next to his new friend on that warm August night, feeling comfort from her and the hopeful thought of reuniting with his lover and wife, Alisha. No longer afraid of dying, no need for struggling to stay alive. He was ready for whatever may come.

"It's a funny thing, Margaret Lynne," he said after a while. "I felt most comfortable with the name Miles when I was struggling for money. Back in the early fifties I sang a little.

"Alisha and I lived down in Memphis, Tennessee, a few blocks from Beale Street where the music was made into records.

"There was just no work to be had, by a black man, anyway. Alisha and I passed by a recordin' studio called Sun Records. There were some groups, trios and such, singin' and recordin' records–black folks, mostly. We stopped and listened one night.

"A white gentleman opened the front door as Alisha and I stood there, and we sang along to the sad song we heard bein' sung inside. "Old Shep." It was about a boy whose dog got old and had to be put out of its misery. The man was the owner, Sam Philips, and he asked if I had any experience in singin'. I told him that I sang in our church choir two nights a week and again on Sundays.

"A'course I hadn't sung in public since I was a boy and that was in church. I didn't tell him that, though. So to make a long story short, he had me audition as a studio singer. Mostly, Maggie, when I sang--and that's if and when I sang–it was as a back-up singer only."

"You're kiddin! You, Curtis Miles, a singer? On records that I've heard?" A funny thing happened as she spoke. Maggie suddenly recalled the boy who lived in a barn behind her house back when she was a kid. She could hear him singing along with the songs on the radio. He seemed to like rhythm and blues. She grinned thinking of the young rube. That's it! *His* name was Miles. The grin melted away as a look of astonishment came over her.

"Maybe you heard my voice. I did a little with the master of the piano, Ivory Joe Hunter, the great Fats Waller, folks like that. Never got to tour with any of 'em. I guess I wasn't that good.

"Made a few bucks until better singers pushed me out. I felt I had a real shot at doing it steady. My voice thought otherwise. It said, "Nice try, Curtis, now be on your way." My dream got fulfilled, for a little while anyway. That's my story and I'm stickin' to it."

Maggie forgot about the country boy of her childhood and listened to Curtis. She rested on her elbows in her faded pink silk robe with her legs planted on the second step more than shoulder-length apart. She felt as if she was right there with him, as if they were both young again. Maggie could almost smell the pungent odor of ashtrays filled with old stubbed-out cigarettes, stale beer, cheep wine, and all that goes on in a recording studio. For a brief moment during his story, Maggie became Alisha.

"God, Miles, how I'd loved to have been there for that. Seeing you having the time of your life, singing your heart out in that studio ... It would have been pure bliss for me!"

"Yeah, ma'am. It was fun, but gettin' paid was a whole lot funner. It didn't pay squat." He crushed out the end of his joint discreetly at the base of a mum plant. "There you go, mum. You can thank me later." He turned back to Maggie, now looking so serene and much younger than her age.

He leaned in, hesitated, and then kissed her. She kissed him back. It was gentle and genuine. "Listen," Maggie whispered. "You old fool, I can think of only one reason why an eighty-year-old would plant a kiss on me. You're stoned!"

"Could be, Ms. Maggie, but you're the most beautiful woman I've had the pleasure of knowing." He swallowed hard. "You remind me so much of Alisha Anne. God knows she was my best friend."

Curtis stopped. Tears welled in his eyes and trickled down his gentle brown cheeks to his cleft chin.

He said, "I see her now and then. She's been coming to me at night next to my bed. She's been there for the last–well, since you came here back on the tenth.

"Alisha stands by the bedside and then just as graceful as ever, drifts to the foot of the bed before gliding softly back up along the side, next to my head. She sort of floats ... in mid-air. I never want her to leave.

"She looks so beautiful, Maggie, my hands tremble and I get tears when I see her. There's a white glow around her, yet she's like she was fifty years ago, only more radiant. I could go with her tonight and it would be all right with me."

Though Maggie listened as he spoke, she also focused on Kathryn, back at the morning AA meeting. She was remembering Kathryn's words, and the voices that had been coming to her at Evergreen and also at the House of Serenity.

"I hear you, Miles," she said. "I don't quite know what to say. Maybe I'll sound selfish when I speak, but I've only begun to know you. I don't want you to leave. I need you. You're all I've got.

"When my illness became terminal, friends stopped coming around. The bastards don't even so much as call or email. I guess they're unable to face life's situations. For them reality is what they watch on the goddamned TV."

He looked up when she said TV as if he had something pertinent to add. "Yeah, TV," he said. "You know it's odd, but lately I've been watching reruns of Lawrence Welk."

"Oh, for God's sake, you can't be serious! Jesus, Miles. I thought I had problems." They laughed out loud.

His voice took on a serious tone as he cleared his throat. "The time has come. You gotta tell me what you're doin' here. You ain't told me *jack* about *nothin'!* If you don't play poker, you should take it up. You have a way of sayin' not much! I'm here to listen. I ain't sleepy and the morning is a long way off."

CHAPTER TWELVE

August 13, 2001 - 1:10 AM

After so many long and arduous years with various doctors of psychology, psychiatry, palm readers, toe readers, and numerous life coaches, Maggie was about to embark on her final journey, the journey to the inner self.

It would require a confrontation with her wild and stormy past.

The tide was high, the seas were choppy, the currents strong; it would not be an easy sail, but sail she must if she was to survive the turbulent waters ahead and walk the quiet and peaceful sandy shores of an island paradise. But did she have the strength?

Margaret Lynne began her final session. Her couch was the front stoop of Evergreen Meadows by the Lake. The best analyst in the world was sitting next to her.

"Where do I begin?" She was almost mumbling, yet she continued. "I have some unloading to do. You stop me if it sounds too much like a woe-is-me kind of crappy story. People who talk like that make me sick, you know?"

He nodded, leaned back and settled in.

She began by talking about the last days of her second bad marriage. "The night I dumped my second husband, Darrell Unsell Hartwig, I grabbed the shithead by the ear, yanked his ass out the front door, ran upstairs and chucked his old brown suitcase out of the second floor bedroom window. It bounced and most of his clothing that I packed fell out as it tumbled toward the street. He picked it up, pouted, and paced up the street to the bus stop. That was twenty-some years ago. I was thirty-two.

Curtis asked, "Why'd you kick him out?"

"Be patient, doc. You'll see. I called him 'Duh' for short. He hated the name. I loved watching him squirm and turn red before he'd tell me to stop calling him 'Duh.' As it turned out he was a weakling with the morals of a drug-infested pimp. We were married for five disastrous months.

"When I first met him he was out of work. He had a teaching degree. When he taught, and that was a rarity, he taught World History. He didn't have to plan homework. The book did that for him.

"Darrell worked harder at staying out of work than finding work. He lived off of my income. His best work, if you could call it that, was in bed and even that was rare.

"Oh, the marriage started off okay, at first. I thought I was in love for real this time around. I tried like hell to make *this* one work. I was a fool. I also got pregnant for the second time. Not by him."

Miles listened, saying, "You seem to fall for a certain type of man. You know that, don't you?"

"You noticed that, too?" she said facetiously. "Anyway, six weeks into the marriage we had our first argument. We were making love one night, me on top of him. We were going at it slow and easy until I felt him go limp. He pushed me aside and went into the bathroom. When he came out he said he was tired. *I* wasn't. I wanted more. And I was going to get it!

"'You just lay there then,' I said to him, 'and I'll do all the work.'

"'Then go faster,' he demanded. 'And give me some head.'

"I didn't like his attitude, but I overlooked it because I wanted to get off that night and get off good!

"'No head until you've been real *nice* to me,' I told him. With my hands full of personal lubricant I took his manhood in my ... not-so-tender hands, and by holding tight and pounding it up and down against his scrotum, it began to perk up.

"I quickened the pace. Soon it began to grow thick and erect. I squeezed harder and drove it home, slamming my hands up and down like a jackhammer on cement. He became rock-hard as he lay across our white satin bed sheets.

"He was writhing with delight. 'Duh' had one of those goofy-looking smiles on his face when I positioned myself on top of him and guided his rod to my clitoris.

"I pulled it back and forth, enjoying the warm, erotic feeling as I eased down lower and lower until his joystick was firmly inside of me. I rocked back and forth, pushing hard. Soon I had his head hanging off the far side of the bed as I continued making hard, hot love to him.

"Rocking hard, I grabbed his balls and the base of his penis and squeezed. To my surprise he let out a soft childlike squeal. He squirmed and breathed, 'Tighter, harder, *tighter!*' I squeezed harder with both hands and drove it home harder and faster. My love juices flowed as my body convulsed. I wanted more and more.

"The shuddering started in the pit of my stomach and radiated to my shoulders down to my toes. I stiffened and arched my back as I reached my first climax of the night. Not done, I continued until my folded legs began to cramp up. I grabbed hold of his elbows as I brought my legs out and in front of me as I sat on him feet-first.

"We looked like a human seesaw as we rocked. It wasn't working, though. I dragged him off the bed. He was almost off headfirst anyway. I lay there with my legs dangling over the edge. He stood and wrapped his arms around the cheeks of my butt and pushed upward.

"My sweet pussy was in position for him to slide his piston in and we continued. He slammed his meat deep inside. I was so aroused I could hardly breathe. My cheeks were hot and my chest was heaving as I gasped for air. Two more times I reached orgasm; one after the other.

"He didn't stop for the longest time. Then when he did, he pushed me to the middle of the bed and he lay on top in the old boring missionary position. He went limp again, so I reached down and clamped on to his lump of scrotum and penis like a vice. He hardened again.

"I pulled it out of my vagina and rubbed the head of his moist member hard, up and down and all around my clit. Oh, God, it felt so damned good! I pulled it harder and harder, faster and faster until I climaxed again.

"When I did, I pushed my wet right index finger far up his rectum. He wiggled. I put three fingers up there and he began to moan with joy.

"He rocked me and I him. The bed was bouncing and the springs squeaked so much I thought it was going to bust wide open and throw us to the ceiling. I had him in me as I held his flaming cock with my left hand.

"By that time most of my right hand was shoved as far into his butt-hole as I could get it before he started ramming me faster and harder. I began my final and best orgasm of the night as he let out a loud *'Oh yeah, oh yeah, mother-fuck-Tamara, yeah!'*

"Still in euphoria, I heard what he had said. Shock waves bolted through my body. My fist flew out of his butt-hole so fast I swear it made a sucking noise. I stiffened and rolled fast and he hit the floor moaning. His head bounced against the corner of the nightstand and the lamp fell on his enlarged penis, scorching it with the hot light bulb.

"Blood flowed from his right temple onto the off-white Berber carpeting. He lay there bleeding, cupping his hands around his manhood as it shrunk into his scrotum and all but disappeared. I looked down at the dumb bastard as he curled into a fetal position. Crap oozed out his of his behind. He was a mess.

Curtis looked puzzled. "'Tamara'? What was that about?"

"Tamara was the name of the fourteen-year-old girl who delivered the newspaper. I was enraged, Curtis. Just fucking wild!"

Maggie paused, taking several deep breaths to slow herself down to regain her composure. What on earth had happened to her? The words had just poured out in a torrent. Her hands trembled as she placed them in front of her in a praying manner, and she bowed her head.

Miles watched as she regained her composure. He pursed his lips and swallowed. After taking a deep breath himself, he said to her, "My Lord, girl! There you were, gettin' me all worked up for a woe-is-me tale, and instead you give me a first-hand account of what you and 'Duh' did behind closed doors! Ain't fair tellin' me that stuff when I ain't ready."

He stood up and put a hand on his heart and turned toward the front door. "I'm goin' to get a can of pop and a Payday to regain my composure, girl. Gotta wash down one of those new pills." He turned back to Maggie and asked, "You got the munchies too?"

She nodded. "A Coke, please, thanks. And I haven't had a Payday since I chucked my hash pipe after the Summer of Love in '69."

It wasn't long before he returned with two cans of Coke and a handful of candy bars and two throw pillows. He dropped a pillow in Maggie's lap as he squatted into a sitting position on the steps, using the other pillow for a cushion.

"My butt gets sore sittin' on cement. Don't have the padding there where it used to be," He said. "You have more to say and miles to go, so I'm gonna sit right here with you until you get to the end of the road and tell me why and how you found yourself here next to me on this warm August night. Now, where were we? Oh yes, 'Duh' likes underage girls. What's next?"

CHAPTER THIRTEEN

1:17 AM

Maggie peeled open the wrapper around her Payday and took a small bite before washing it down with the Coke.

"God, Miles," she said, "I can't remember when this tasted *so good.* With the meds the sense of taste ain't what it used to be." She nodded, adding, "Ya?"

He acknowledged her nod with his own. "Ya, I know. At my age a fried horse turd wouldn't taste much different than an Oscar Meyer wiener."

"Jesus, Miles!" She took a sip of Coke, replaying his remark about horse turds. She began to laugh and cough at the same time. Wiping her nose with her sleeve as Coke dribbled from her nostrils, she couldn't stop laughing.

Curtis Miles smiled as he watched her hysterics. He put his forefinger to his lips. "Shh, don't wake up the ghosts around here." She stopped laughing.

After settling down, she picked up where she'd left off, telling him about the dissolution of her second and last marriage.

The day she chucked old Darrell Unsel Hartwig's suitcase out of the upstairs window was a culmination of the deep disgust she harbored toward men, especially her second and final husband. It happened when she walked home from the museum.

Giving a talk to second graders had been fun for Maggie. With the kids in a half circle, she sat on a small stool in front of them as she told of a large bone that she and her colleagues unearthed in New Mexico. A dinosaur bone of great significance was passed around so all the children could touch and feel it. They had a field day at the museum where Maggie was working as the curator.

"You're holding a bone that's over 159 million years old," she said. "It's even older than your grandparents," she chuckled. "This is a leg bone of the Coelophysis, one of the very oldest of dinosaurs. We found it at a place called Ghost Ranch."

Maggie watched in delight as the children squirmed and whispered to one another. "Yes, Ghost Ranch is a real place in the county of Rio Arriba, New Mexico. The first bones of its kind were discovered in the nineteen-forties. Not *that* long ago, really," she added.

"My day ended earlier than usual," she now told Curtis. "It was a warm, sunny summer day. I'd walked the six and a half blocks to the museum.

"I closed and locked the door to the museum at one-fifteen and made it to the front door of my house less than fifteen minutes later.

"'Duh' usually took a nap around this time of day when he wasn't working, which was most of the time. The sun was glaring through the front window over the couch. I placed a knee on the couch and leaned over to close the drapes. There was an old, faded black Buick out front, parked at the curb. Nothing out of the ordinary; cars parked up and down the street every day.

"I turned from the window to sit down when I happened to notice a magazine that had fallen behind the couch on the floor. Reaching for it, I placed it on top of the others on the end table, picked up the remote, and turned on the TV. Glancing at the rescued magazine on top of the others, something caught my eye. It begged for more attention.

"It wasn't mine. I thumbed through it. While turning the pages, I stopped, studying one model in an unusual pose. He wore his blond hair short and was baring his hairless chest. All he wore was black Western leather gloves with knotted streamers above his wrists and a

78

gun belt. He held a pair of silver six-shooters in his hands and was pointing them at the camera.

"Just below the holsters a thin lace of leather was tied around each leg, holding the holsters in place.

"The young hairless model exposed himself to the world. He couldn't have been more than sixteen years old. I flipped it over to the cover. It read in large print: *Guy Magazine,* and below the naked male model it continued in small print, 'For the Discreet Gentleman.' By the tattered appearance and pages stuck together, I knew it'd been around awhile.

"I slipped it in the magazine rack. With the remote in hand I flicked on the TV and hit the mute button. I was in a spiraling daze. I sat numb, staring at the silent TV.

"That's when it happened. I heard a rustling sound upstairs, then voices. The voices became louder, more boisterous and playful. The laughter moved along the upstairs hallway echoing toward the staircase.

"My husband and another man made their way down the steps, jostling and grabbing at one another.

"Naked, Darrell grabbed his mate and put him in a headlock as they set foot on the floor, bending him over and pulling him along.

"The older, taller man appeared helpless until he reached and clutched onto Darrell's crotch. They staggered together toward the living room on their way to the kitchen, as Darrell eased his grip on the man and let go of him. The man squeezed harder on Darrell, who said, 'You're hurting me, Larry. Ease up.'

"The man sneered at him, and then smacked his bare butt, hard.

"Here's the kicker, Miles. Dr. Fleming brings up the name, Bishop Paul Cheney and some guy named Lawrence Burke, and connects them with 'Duh,' yet I just draw a blank every time. I feel an emptiness when I hear it and I block it out. Now, I think that there *is* a correlation somewhere between those guys, 'Duh,' and me.

"Dr. Fleming told me that Paul Cheney had been the Bishop here in Capital City when I was growing up, about an hour from here. He also had a young friend named Lawrence Burke. A priest. Remember when I told you about old Raymond and Burke?

"Anyway, we lived–I mean my family lived–in a big two story white-framed farmhouse. I remember that now, Miles. Why now? Right *now* as we speak?" Maggie asked.

"Don't know, but it's time, girl," he replied.

"My God! This is incredible!" she exclaimed. "I'm getting images that I haven't seen before. Or if I have, I'd forgotten them. It's like shards of my past flashing and settling inside my brain. I can't explain it."

"Talk it out girl," he said. "Talk it out loud to me. So what happened with 'Duh' and Larry?"

She sighed. "They walked right in front of me as they glanced at the TV. It was then that Darrell saw me and was startled, to say the least.

"Guys?" I asked. "Guys? Darrell, I'm not going to *compete* for your affection. Not with a young girl, not with an old man. I can't share you with another, any more than you could share your nuts with a squirrel."

"Our daughter Bliss was still at summer camp. I told him I'd leave. Then I stopped in mid-sentence and said, 'No, *you* will leave this house before she gets back.' He did.

"Miles. Ever stood in your living room feeling like two cents and having an argument with two naked men, one being your husband?"

"Can't say I have," he said, stifling a chuckle as he opened up a second Payday and took a bite.

She shook her head, saying, "I can't believe I was so blind, so stupid, so much in denial! Mad as hell, I grabbed the keys and got in our car. I don't know where I went but I was gone for about an hour, just driving. When I came back, the big Buick was gone. His buddy had dressed and fled. And on the infamous magazine 'Duh' had laid a rosary.

"Outraged at his lethargic and feel-sorry-for-me look, I started packing his things. He knew the end of our marriage was near. He just didn't realize *how* near.

"The only time I saw him again was at the courthouse, when he was with his lawyer, and I was with mine. He always found a way to cut at my heart. He leaned over to me as we waited in the hallway during a short recess and whispered, "My dying wish is to be found dead in a cave while screwing dozens of little girls."

"Girls?" asked Curtis with a raised eyebrow.

"Go figure. Somehow he got involved with the FLDS. That's the Fundamental Latter Day Saints, where one guy has a bunch of wives and kids.

"Maybe it has something to do with history. He didn't give diddly about now–the present, I mean. When he had something of value to say, it was about the past only. As if *now* was not happening. Strange man, that dude."

"You're making progress, woman. Let's go back a bit further and tell me about your first husband and how you met him."

"Hm." She shook her head as she recalled. "We met at a tailgating party in the parking lot of a tavern. It was across the street from Camp Randall Stadium, where the Wisconsin Badgers played football. I'll never forget the front of the building. It's made out of brick and stone and housed the basketball team. The address is ingrained in my head: 1440 Monroe Street.

"Near the top of the building was an old, very faded red W. Why they never repainted it I'll never know. Guess they didn't have as much pride as they claimed to. I haven't been there in decades. We were visiting.

"My sorority sisters and I were standing outside of a bar called Jingles, drinking beer from plastic cups. It was a beautiful Wisconsin fall day. Cool, partly cloudy, jeans and sweater weather.

"That's when I met Raymond. He stood about five feet ten. Kept giving me the eye.

"He was cocky, witty and smiled. I liked him. He had short dark hair growing thin. He came over and struck up a conversation with me, talking a-mile-a-minute. Before I knew it, Miles, we fell in love. I had his baby in my junior year. We married in the summer. My father Ed held her in his arms the day we were married.

"Graduation day was a year away for both of us. Raymond was working part time with the Wisconsin Bell telephone company. He did his studying while working the third shift at the central office, just a few blocks from campus.

"He didn't go back to school his senior year; instead he went to work full time with the company and was making fair wages and good benefits. Said he couldn't pass up the money. He knew everything–just ask him. I, on the other hand, tended the baby, finished school, and got my degree in Anthropology and a minor in Archeology.

"My work often took me away from the college town and he stayed home with Bliss, our daughter. He handed her off to my parents out in the country. When I came back I took the role of mother, housewife, and head wage-earner.

"Raymond Polanski couldn't tell the truth, much less run a farm, though he tried and lost a bundle of money in the process, mostly mine.

"He blamed the loss of the farm on me. He thought that I should have helped him with the planting of the crops and so on.

"There I was, doing what I went to school for, digging up bones and he tried to be a telephone man *and* a Wisconsin dirt farmer. Needless to say, it didn't work out. He never had time for our daughter–or me, for that matter. His bright witticisms soon turned to dark sarcasm and I became the butt of his jokes. He came home late and lied about where he'd been. He loved only himself. It was time to leave.

"I found solace in a co-worker and so did he. He wasn't a good father at all. He never read to her, or took her anywhere unless I urged him.

Curtis Miles listened intensely. "Did he help at *all* with raising or teaching Bliss?"

"Never changed a diaper as far as I know. Oh well, I accept half of the blame. But Bliss was so precious. We divorced. He never paid alimony nor child support. I don't know where the hell he went and I don't care. It's as if he dropped off the face of the earth. So fuck him, too.

"That's another thing, Miles. I don't know *where* she is. I've lost contact with her. Here I am dying and I can't find her to tell her!"

Maggie shook from head to toe and then broke down and wept. Curtis held her. He did his job. It was what he'd been sent to do.

She opened up as they sat out on the steps on that sultry August night, pushing toward a morning of reckoning.

It was getting late; he had to ask one more question.

"What about the child? You said you were pregnant when you married, or after you married, 'Duh.'"

"I love you, Curtis Miles." She wiped her tears as she leaned away from his comforting arms and shoulder. "Too much for me right now," she said. "Maybe I can get some sleep and go to another meeting later on this morning."

Curtis was silent. He studied her as she got to her feet and walked to the front door. He shook his head knowing that God has plans that sometimes–well, most of the time–differs from ours. "Be out front, Maggie. I'll be by same time as tonight."

CHAPTER FOURTEEN

1:50 AM

S huffling in from outside, near the front desk, Maggie felt a wisp of cold air. The hair on the back of her neck stood on end.

The small lamp was lit. A partially crushed cigarette butt lay in the dark plastic ashtray. It was still smoldering, smoke spiraling up toward the light. *Lena doesn't smoke*, she thought. *Never smelled it on her, anyway. Maybe it's that asshole, Gunderson. Anything's possible.* Too tired to investigate, she traipsed to her room, closing the door behind her. She undressed in front of the mirror.

***

Kurt Gunderson sat on an old wooden chair in the old wine cellar below the kitchen. Holding the phone receiver to one ear as he listened, he held a plain white envelope in the other hand.

"Your professionalism with Fleming was … admirable. I've arrived at my final destination. There's much to accomplish here. You'll be an asset to the final solution. We've been keeping tabs on this woman for too long. It's time to end it.

"It's the same tooth as Fleming's, Kurt. I don't want anything to get in the way of our progress. The one-way ticket should be in your possession as we speak. The FLOC is in business and business is good."

***

She lay naked atop the sheets in her dark room on the first floor. There was no window for a breeze to comfort her. A hundred scenes had entered her mind. She had pierced the veil to her past, revealing all the horrific details of the lost days Dr. Fleming had wanted to her to find. She grew tired as her mind raced. She could see the farmhouse where she grew up and her loving parents, Ed and Helen Hornsby.

Timothy Lee was on the new swing set in the backyard. Mrs. Kathryn Knee pushed him from behind. She also remembered William, the big stocky fourteen-year-old who lived behind them, just beyond the field of rye. He slept in the barn. His father whipped him unmercifully. For that the town Sheriff arrested him and put him in jail.

William stayed at her house for Christmas that year. The boy dreamed of being a back-up singer in a rhythm and blues band. His name was William Miles Messenger.

Her eyelids grew heavy.

The memories of those three missing days had come back. She remembered all the gory details. Maggie took no medicine that night and cried herself to sleep.

It was a restless sleep. She tossed and turned and her dreams were frightening. She awoke screaming. Startled, she sat on the edge of the bed catching her breath and clearing her thoughts.

Her mouth was dry. She had to pee. Returning from the bathroom, she glanced at her watch: 4:29 AM. She couldn't sleep. She wanted air. With her white cotton robe around her shoulders, she padded out of her room barefoot and up the hallway to the front entrance.

The light was now turned off at the front desk on her left. She could smell the stale odor of crushed cigarettes. The fax machine was spitting out an eight-and-a-half-by-eleven.

Suddenly she heard a noise at the front door. Her heart pounding, she thought of racing back to her room, yet she was curious. She pulled the robe around her tight and folded her arms. Someone was making a poor attempt to unlock the door. Maggie stepped to the side of the door and stood, listening.

"Why me all the time? I just get done with a double shift at the hospital and good old Lena sends me a fax saying she's going away for a few days. Lena never went anywhere in her *life* except the convent. Morris, for chrissake, you gave me the wrong set of keys." She tried another. This time the lock rolled as the key did a one-eighty.

Holding the door ajar with her foot she bent down, picked up the paper grocery bag, and pushed herself inside. The door closed by itself. The woman, dressed in a white short sleeve shirt with khaki shorts and sandals, walked over to the desk and set the bag down. "Whew." All at once she felt uneasy. Turning toward the door, she saw a shadow.

"You must be Nurse Chloe," Maggie said. "Why four-thirty?"

Startled, she said, "Damn, you scared the shit out of me. You're Maggie, I take it?"

"I am."

Chloe walked Maggie down the side hallway between the front desk and her room. Beyond the dining hall she shoved the door open and flipped on the lights in the old outdated kitchen. "How do you like your tea?" she asked.

"With ice, and a friend." Maggie responded.

"Me too. You know why I'm here?"

"I do."

Chloe put the contents of her grocery bag into the refrigerator and poured water and a few tablespoons of instant tea into a pitcher and added sugar. A few minutes later they sat sipping iced tea at an old oak table that overlooked the back of the building and the dried-up swamp where the lake used to be.

With a perplexed look Maggie said, "Lena never said a word to me about leaving. Did I miss something? I thought she was an up-and-down gal."

"Me too. Unless ..."

"Unless what?" Maggie asked.

"Unless Mother Superior called her back to Madison."

Maggie's jaw dropped. "She's a goddamn nun?"

"Uh, I don't think she's a *goddamn* nun, but she *is* a Carmelite, and has been assigned here for the past several years. Jacqueline is the name she took, though lately she prefers her given name. I think she's rethinking the whole matter. She's got a heart of gold, so maybe it's a menopausal thing.

Maggie nodded. "Maybe."

"She'll turn up," Chloe said. "Lena's not one to leave her post. The tea all right?"

"No," Maggie responded. "Tastes like I made it. I'm not a good tea maker."

"Thanks a heap. Next time it's your turn." Chloe said. "You smell smoke?

Maggie sniffed and said, "Yeah, why?"

"It's just a question," Chloe said. "I smell it back here in the kitchen once in awhile.

Maggie felt comfortable with Chloe. She gave her a brief synopsis of why she was there, guessing that Chloe knew only what Dr. Betz had sent to Dr. Gallagher. "By the way, what do you know of the janitor here?"

"Gunderson? Haven't really seen him, much less talk to him." She said, "Mo, my boss, Morris Gallagher, doesn't trust him for some reason. I figure the less I see or hear of him, the better."

"I get the same feeling," Maggie said with a sigh.

"And, ah, your memory?" Chloe asked.

Maggie slouched and said, "So you got Fleming's report as well?"

"Yup," Chloe said, "the whole shebang."

Maggie pursed her lips, paused and said, "Well, since you brought it up, I *have* regained some, lots, yup–right down to the kidnapping. My brother and I."

Chloe shot her a look.

CHAPTER FIFTEEN

5:01 AM - Tea, Mrs. Knee and Me

Maggie's mind was rolling. The words came faster than she could think. "We were kidnapped. I never told him. I had a shrink-he sent me here. I mean–I told him everything I could remember. Since I've been journaling, things have been happening. Bits and pieces have come back since I met Curtis."

"You mean Kurt? Kurt Gunderson?" Chloe was confused.

"No, not Gunderson, I mean Curtis Presley, the caretaker or whatever he is here. The old guy who takes me to the AA meetings and talks with me at night."

Chloe furled her eyebrows, "You have a ... visitor?"

"Yeah. Don't look so surprised. Lena's the one who called him to take me to the meetings. I remember it from my first day here. At least I'm pretty sure that's how he came to pick me up. So, yes, I have a night visitor. We talk for hours out on the front steps. We were there last night, until the wee hours of the morning. We talked about lots of things, both of us."

Chloe held her glass with both hands and pushed back on her chair. "Then who's Miles?"

"Curtis–Curtis Miles Presley. It's a long story," she said.

"I've read that from Lena's reports." Chloe said.

"I suppose she said that I talk to myself, and see and hear things. And that I swear like a drunken sailor. She mention that?"

Lifting her cold glass of tea to her lips Chloe smiled and said, "She did."

"Well, there you have it then. I swear, going crazy *and* dying at the same time." Maggie took another sip and set the cup down hard on the table.

"I don't think you're crazy," Chloe said. "You're tough. You're a survivor, a strong woman. Maybe you just need closure on something, that's all."

Maggie took a deep breath and said, "Did you know that I was born not far from here and lived in a farm house with my younger brother? Down the road from the old one-room Penn Hollow schoolhouse."

Chloe said, "I've got time, Maggie. I'm happy to listen. Something about you makes me feel ... at home. She flipped off her sandals and put her feet on the cool cement floor as Maggie opened up, going over the things that came out a few hours earlier with Curtis.

"... and Timmy and I were sitting in the living room by the Christmas tree that my dad had just put up. We breathed in the aroma of the fresh cut fir and imagined Santa sitting there with us, when the front door opened.

"We turned to see who it was. The strange man in black frightened us. There was no smile, just a stern look. He seemed to stare right through us. He made me feel guilty as hell about something, though I had no reason to be. He stretched and grabbed our arms, pulling us off the floor.

"It hurt like hell. He sped away with us in his car on the floor of the front seat. Timmy was crying. I put my arms around him, hugging him for the whole ride to the man's house. He called us bad names. He said I was a dirty, filthy whore.

"'Am not,' I said. 'I'm *not* a dirty whore. I'm clean.' I was barely eight at the time. Timmy was six. For some reason the man didn't scare me enough to keep my mouth shut.

I spoke up for myself, always have, always will. He kept us in an upstairs room for several days, tied and taped to a bed. Timmy and I thought we'd die from hunger. There was a chamber pot under the bed. The man and his young pock-marked friend untied us so Timmy and I could use it, and empty it.

"Oh, my God, Chloe. I remember his friend now, yet I can't picture his face except the pockmarks, or hear his voice. I just remember how he made me feel. The bastard was a cold-hearted sonofabitch. A fucking pedophile he was, the cocksucker."

"Tell me about him," Chloe pleaded, "Don't hold back."

Maggie continued. "The tall fuck would come into our room late at night. He'd lie between Timmy and me.

"We had no clothes except what we were wearing when the man took us from our house. That man was a bishop, a Catholic fucking bishop, Paul Cheney. He put white linen smock-things on us. I think they were part of an altar boy's vestments. The damn things were about three feet too long. We rolled 'em up and managed somehow.

"The special *friend* of the bishop would sneak into our room late at night. Timmy slept right through it. Unlike Timmy, I was wide awake when he came in and slipped into our bed. He pulled my nightgown up to my chin. I could feel his big hand make its way all over my body. He touched my vagina."

"Oh, God, Maggie." Chloe shook her head. "I just can't imagine."

She nodded and continued. "He played there for a long time. Then he rubbed my butt as he fingered around my vagina. He tried to put it in me, but I pushed it away. It hurt. He'd make me touch him. I mean He forced my hand on his cock.

"He tried to get me to jack him off, but I played stupid. I didn't want to touch the groady old thing. It felt *dirty* touching him. He tried to make a game out of it. I wasn't going for it, and he got pissed every time."

"Jee-zus! What a sick bastard." Chloe said, shaking her head.

"One night he scared the hell out of me. Timmy was sound asleep. The bastard came into the room with a strange smirk on his face. My body trembled.

"That night he stood next to the bed as he fondled me. He was naked and his penis seemed huge from my point of view, lying on the bed, just inches away from the damn thing. I remember being petrified!

"Then I noticed he had something in his hand. He was up to something–I didn't know what yet. Christ. I was just eight years old, Chloe. Eight!"

"Oh, Maggie, that must have been terrifying. What were you thinking while that was going on?" she asked.

"I kept asking myself, what's he going to do to me? It didn't take long to find out. He walked around to the other side of the bed and pulled the sheets aside and he unwrapped the thing in his hand. It was butter. A goddamn stick of butter! He smeared some of it on his penis and some on Timmy's behind. He pulled Timmy up to him.

"He tried to enter Timmy, who was still asleep. He screamed. Frightened, I pulled on Timmy's arm and he put him back on the bed. He rubbed his eyes as I told him that everything was all right and that he'd just had a bad dream.

"He went back to sleep. He never knew what happened. The sicko stepped over to me. It was my turn. This time he sat on the side of the bed. I knew what he wanted. To protect Timmy, I obeyed his commands. He sat me on his lap, naked."

"The dirty bastard, Maggie!" Chloe reached over and held Maggie's hand as she continued.

"I eased down with his dick between my legs. He held tight to me as he pushed and pulled me up and down. He tried like hell to enter my vagina, but I wouldn't let him. His penis slid through my legs, and that's *all* it did.

"Then, from out of nowhere, something that looked like a greenish ball appeared and hovered in a corner of the room. At the same time a car pulled up the driveway. There was a knock on the front door. The bishop answered it as the priest pushed me away, and slipped out of the bedroom. It saved my brother *and* my virginity. The round green color faded away. I can't tell you what it was, but I felt comforted by it.

"Now that's the first time I told anyone about that episode in my life. Curtis helped me a lot, dredging up this long-ago, forgotten stuff. I call him my midnight therapist."

"Sounds like a wonderful guy," Chloe replied.

"Oh he is, Chloe! He's special. A good man, bad ticker and all."

"So, want to tell me how you and your brother got out of there? I mean what happened after that night? You got free somehow." Chloe was digging, stirring, and probing. It was working.

"We got out. That's all I can say right now. Here's the kicker. After Curtis Miles and I talked, I went to bed without any meds and I had some bad dreams. Couldn't sleep-two hours at most. That's when I went to the front door. I was going out for fresh air when you were fumbling with the keys outside. Do you know you talk to yourself?"

Before Chloe could respond, Maggie picked up her story where she had left off. Once again the long-forgotten, dark memories came flooding back.

"Anyway, the bishop put us in his car and drove us here, Chloe. Right *here*, for God's sake! We were being held on the third floor, I think." Maggie's eyes widened in disbelief as a new memory came to her. "A *nun* brought us food–breakfast, anyway. I'm sorry, but it gets a bit fuzzy in the details. We were here one or two nights. There were *two* nuns, now I recall–a large nun and a skinny one. One of them dressed us, and put makeup and wigs on us the last night we were here.

"I remember being tied to a chair, Timmy and I. We were sitting on a kind of stage with the wigs, lipstick, and makeup. There were voices--a lot of men in the dimly lit room, we could barely see them.

"It was dark and smoky. We were scared out of our wits when all of a sudden, something strange took place. I don't know how to explain it. A bright light came from above. Then, all of a sudden, a man in a red suit stood between Timmy and me. Yes, I know what you're thinking, Chloe."

Chloe rested an arm on the table, as she was about to say, "Sa–?"

"It *was* Santa Claus. I don't know how the hell we got back home, but we did. I must have blacked out and dreamt that Santa saved us. I just don't know about that part.

"Gordon Maxwell, the sheriff of Pine Nut, was involved in it. I remember, Chloe, I remember his name. My folks talked about the newspaper stories of him and my schoolteacher Kathryn Knee breaking up a child-smuggling ring. Oh, my God, Chloe! There was a big bust, right here in this goddamned building!"

Chloe hung on every word. "Here?"

Maggie nodded. "Dr. Fleming will be proud of me," she said, smiling. "I'll have to call him and tell him of the progress I've been making. I'm exhausted."

But Maggie wasn't finished. She went on to tell Chloe all the things that she had blocked from her memory. She threw in the two bad marriages and Dr. Betz's diagnosis. She talked about her stormy relationship with her daughter, how Bliss joined the Marine Corps and stayed in for almost nine years.

Chloe was a good listener. She had to be. It was her job. Someone had to tell Maggie about Dr. Fleming, though. Was she the one? Was now the right time to tell her, the right place—in the kitchen at five-thirty in the morning? Dr. Morris Gallagher could tell her, but he had a full schedule and wasn't particularly good with that sort of thing anyway.

Chloe pushed away from the table and said, "Good idea, Maggie. Hey, I'm going to take a shower and get ready for the day. What say I make breakfast? We can continue with our conversation. This time I'll talk. I have something that you'll want to hear. It may be time for your medication."

"Why?" Maggie asked.

Chloe didn't know what to say. Should Maggie be medicated before or after hearing about Dr. Fleming?

"I lied. There is something else that I haven't told you—told anyone, not even my husbands or my daughter, Bliss." Maggie leaned against the doorjamb with folded arms as she watched the svelte, long-legged nurse with short auburn hair, rinse the glasses at the sink. Chloe turned in her direction.

"When I was about thirty-ish, I got pregnant again. Alone, I was confused. I wanted to keep it. The nuns at the hospital talked me out of it. They said I'd live with 'my mistake'—their words, not mine—the rest of my life. It wouldn't be good for her sister, the baby, or me.

"I gave the baby up through the only agency I knew, the National Adoption Association in Chicago. I had a healthy, beautiful, baby girl. They let me hug her and kiss her. I cried for days–months afterward." Maggie began to sob. "I pray every day that she's had a good life."

Chloe, with wet hands and all, reached out to Maggie, consoling the sobbing woman. She too, had tears. Chloe held her tight saying, "They say that only rich people adopted back in the day. Perhaps she had a loving family."

CHAPTER SIXTEEN

6:14 AM - A Couple of Miles Away

"Oh, hi, Delores. Sorry, I thought I called Mick's phone. I did? He took the red-eye? Oh, he knew I'd call? Sure, I'll pick him up, no problem." Gordon flipped his phone shut and put it back in his pocket.

Kathryn was nearby. "You coming back this way or do you want me to ride along?"

"We'll stop back," he said. "Damn it. He always knows everything *first!* And I can't get Aaron on the line either." Gordon fumbled with the keys and change in his pocket. "It's quarter past six. You going to write or take your morning walk?"

"Walk."

Driving to the airport in a rented Ford Taurus, Gordon thought about his and Mick's first caper.

It was here that Gordon was forced to face his demons. His one-year stint at the Capital City Minor Seminary for Boys was no picnic.

He was "the chosen one" for some sick and demented rituals by perverted priests. He wasn't alone. Worse yet, some kids had disappeared. That's when the place was shut down–for a while, anyway, before the diocese reopened it as a retirement home for priests and to serve the surrounding community, a small portion of space was used as a retreat center, open to the public, more or less.

It was renamed Evergreen Meadows by the Lake. "By the lake" was dropped when it went dry after corporate farmers used up most of the ground water for irrigation. When Gordon was a seminarian, the area was the football field and baseball diamond. Now it's a goddamn mud hole. At least that's what he'd heard. He'd always thought about going back and seeing it for himself. Now he *had* to.

Little Margaret Lynne was in danger. And like fifty-some years before, she was once again in the same building-and in serious trouble. Mickey told him so late last night. Kat was right. She's always right. Women. How do they always know?

He took the airport exit. As it looped around, he eased off the gas pedal. A thin, wiry guy stood holding the handle of a small, dark-blue carry-on at the curb, smiling. He wasn't alone.

A puddle of water filled a small portion of the gutter from an early morning rain. Gordon pulled over to the curb, splashing water on the man's wingtips.

The slight-built man tapped his shoes to get the rainwater off and said, "Hey, old man, I could use a lift."

"Always bitchin' about your height," Gordon said with a straight face as he jumped out of his car. Noticing the colorful woman standing next to him, he asked, "New roommate?" He popped the trunk lid from the driver's side door panel. Mickey placed his carry-on and his companion's suitcase inside and slid into the back seat.

Mickey said, "Gordy, this is M.G., Dr. Betz's nurse. She came out from Phoenix to see Maggie. I met her at the airport."

Gordon glanced in the rearview mirror, eying the two and nodding to M.G. Gordon was silent. He glanced at Mickey again via the rearview as he pulled away from the curb. He winked.

"Good to see you, you old fart," Mickey said. "Listen, is there a coffee shop around here someplace? I'm starved. Nothing was served on the plane. Could use donuts or cinnamon rolls. I'll buy."

"*You'll* buy? You haven't bought since the Cubs were in the World Series. And why don't you have your cell phone with you? Had a nice conversation with Delores a few minutes ago."

"Got a new one. An iPhone. I'm an Apple man, now. Less crashes, no virus problems. We gotta talk, buddy."

M.G. followed Gordon's eyes as he studied her through the mirror. She looked away through the window at the surroundings and said, "Hey. I know this place. There's a little strip mall just a few minutes from here and they have a quaint little outdoor café, the Hula Java."

Gordon's right eyebrow lifted a millimeter, just enough for her to notice.

"I googled it," she explained.

He frowned.

Mickey laughed out loud. "Sorry, old man. Had to laugh. She's all right. We know each other. She's got a dark side, though, FBI trainee dropout."

"Not exactly," M.G. pointed out. You might say I work under contract. I have a specialty. Sickos. God's mistakes. You know, neo-Nazi bloodsuckers that buy and sell kids."

Gordon nodded. "So, what were you doing in a doctor's office in Scottsdale?"

She shot Mickey a glance, then turned back to Gordon and said, "Took a side job. Insurance. The Feds were looking into Dr. B.'s insurance methods. Boring stuff, really. They paid me big bucks, so what the hell..."

"Was he scamming?" Gordon asked.

"Not any more than the others," she lied. Insurance had nothing to do with it. A cover is a cover is a cover.

***

It was another hazy August morning in the Midwest. They sat outside. The twenty-ish cook and sole waitress were bored. The pimply-faced overweight waitress dressed in black with a butterfly tattoo flying across her cleavage moaned, "Fuckin' old people."

Her lips and ears had multiple piercings and two big black pearls impaled on her tongue. Occasionally she'd stick out her tongue and click them on her teeth. It drove Gordon nuts.

"I just googled this place. It didn't say how the service was," M.G. said as she shrugged.

Just down the road Mick graduated from his first undercover operation. Gordon was a sheriff then and played it straight up. They had a lot to catch up on but there was a sense of urgency now. Margaret Lynne was in danger, they know, whether she knew it or not.

"Remember this place, Gordy old boy? You *pointed* your finger at me!"

Gordon grunted. "Worked out, didn't it?"

"Just the same. That why you left the badge and side arm behind, to go on the talk circuit?

"Yup." Gordon sometimes carried a Walther P-38, whether Mickey knew it or not. He shot a glance at his pal.

"I've worked with M.G. in the past," Mickey said, "though I'd never actually met her. Has something beyond a woman's intuition. Does things to get her man that other agents can't. Law is just a suggestion to her."

Gordon shifted his eyebrows. The goth-looking waitress stood next to him. "Plain bagel, no butter; coffee and water," he told her.

She clicked her pearls on her teeth and asked, "Are you Jewish?"

"I'm circumcised, does that count?" Gordon remained motionless as his eyes turned to M.G. to get a reaction. There was none.

"What's your name?" M.G. asked the waitress, who shifted from one foot then the other before replying, "Shirley."

"Shirley, I'd like a glass of pineapple juice and a raisin bagel, toasted and sliced."

"Got it." Turning to Mickey, she looked down and over her reading glasses. "What about you? Need more time?"

"Ah ... no, I was hoping for a glazed donut."

"Sugar donuts. We got sugar donuts. Too hot and humid for glazed," she said with another aggravating click of pearls on teeth.

"Four, then, and a cup of coffee," he said.

"Comin' up," Shirley said as she turned and waddled to the open door and placed their order. The cook had overheard and was already pouring the drinks.

"Now," Gordon said, heaving a deep sigh, "about Richard."

Mickey told him what he knew. "I've been in touch with the Phoenix FBI agents. Someone tried to make it look like a patient had gone berserk and strangled him. Didn't go down that way. Coroner found a crown missing from the first quadrant, second tooth. Radio signal. One more thing. He had a stab wound in his neck."

"Makes no sense, Mick," Gordon said. "If he's dead he wouldn't be going anywhere."

Mickey nodded. "Whoever it was knew he was an agent or former agent. Looks like an inside job. Someone who knew about radio signals and GPS implants."

"In their teeth?" Gordon asked. "But why take it? He's dead. Unless it was going to be reprogrammed for someone else."

"Possibly the killer's signature, you know?" Mickey tapped his fingers on the plastic table.

"Bingo," M.G. chimed in. "Two needle marks found behind his right ear. They're doing an autopsy. Someone, probably two working together, put him to sleep, permanently before he was strangled, or at the same time so he wouldn't put up a fight."

"That would explain the last text I got," Gordon said. "It was from Richard but it was strange. Started out okay, but dissolved into gibberish, like a *lot* of K's. He was in the middle of a sentence, Mick, which means he died while texting me. He *knew* I was coming here, though. You and he were pretty good buds, ya?"

Mickey nodded, saying, "We kept in touch. Checked on mutual friends, you know how it is."

Shirley waddled out with the orders. She got it right.

"Who wanted him dead? And why?" Gordon was stumped. He turned and asked, "Excuse me for asking, but is M.G. your code name or–"

"Morning Glory. I changed my given name to Morning Glory back in my college days. It's a long story, but M.G. is easier on everybody, including me.

"So, you're on ... contract?" Gordon wanted to know more.

"Yes. I have associates. They're my family. A common thread connects us. Our ties are thicker than blood, united, victims-once–never-again kind of thing. When one of us is called into action, we all play a part. We have certain skills that make us independent of one another. We take no prisoners. We never lose." She spoke in a monotone voice. Cool and collected.

"The agency knows us," she continued. "We don't cross lines. It's about boundaries. That's why I work only when asked. Quantico doesn't know about me, at least not on paper. There's no thumbprint, picture or signature of mine in Virginia. I don't exist."

"I hear this, M.G., but tell me again why you came here to see Margaret." He wanted the whole story, but doubted he'd get it. He was right.

"Twenty questions, huh? Been assigned to Dr. Aaron Betz for the past couple of months. The agency set it up. They were watching him and one of his patients for something more than insurance fraud, but kept me out of the loop.

"They worry about me. Think I might take the law into my own hands. Arizona is a place where manslaughter is like a three-thousand-dollar fine and a suspended five-year sentence. Some cases, anyway.

"It's a tax-cut state. Murder is an everyday event. Gunfights are nightly fare. Makes the gunfight at the OK Corral look like childs play.

"Anyway," she went on, "a while ago your Margaret came in. I know her as Maggie. According to the files she was being treated for exhaustion. That was before Betz saw her and found the cancer. He's been treating her by the book, giving her the proper medication. It's been bugging me, though. She doesn't react to the meds like his other patients. She's been seeing Dr. Fleming, so I kept my hands off.

"When I got the news about him, I felt bad for her–and sad for Fleming, of course. He was like a father to me. The FBI ran a check on his cell phone. He was texting you. They contacted me about it, as well as Mickey here. We never met in person until today. So here we are."

Mickey took notes as she talked. He had a fast brain. He could have been a professional gambler or a scam artist, and always kept two steps ahead of everyone else. His memory bank was opening files, checking and cross-checking Aaron Betz.

He got up and asked Gordon for the keys. He opened the trunk and took out his Mac Book. He had to find out for sure. Something was amiss and he knew it.

Gordon glanced at M.G. while Mickey was engrossed in his files. "Shirley," Gordon waved at the waitress sitting at the counter with the cook, smoking a cigarette. She placed the fag between the lips of the cook and waddled out with the bill, tongue wagging, pearls clicking. Gordon did everything he could from reaching in and ripping them out of her tongue, one by one. He paid the tab—as usual.

***

At 7:10 AM she heard the car drive up. Peering out the window of the motel, Kat smiled as she saw Mickey Zaugbaum leap from the back door and rush to the other side to open the door for M.G. Kat's brows furled. She stepped outside to greet them.

"M.G., my wife, Kat," Gordon said. They shook hands.

Mickey wormed his way between them and gave Kat a big long hug. "You get better lookin' every day, girl. Can't talk now. Gotta look somethin' up." He proceeded inside the room, set his laptop on the table-desk and went to work.

"M.G. is Maggie's nurse out in Scottsdale," Gordon explained. "She was a good friend of Dick Fleming. She came out to visit Maggie. Remember the text message I got from Richard? It was his last message. He was murdered as he sent it. Somebody strangled him in his office. You know the story."

Kat frowned. "Wish Lloyd was around."

Gordon jingled the change in his pocket as he felt a lump in his throat. "Those were the good old days, dear. I miss 'em, too. Best barber and the craftiest set-up man I ever worked with."

CHAPTER SEVENTEEN

Evergreen Meadows - 7:12 AM

"I'm not dizzy and I don't feel faint. Really, I'd prefer not to," Maggie said.

Chloe set the carton of milk on the dresser and the cup of pills next to it. "Sit down, Maggie. I have something to tell you."

Maggie stood at the side of her bed as Chloe leaned against the small dresser against the wall. "Is it my health? If that's what you want to tell me, I know I don't have–"

"Sit down!"

Taken back, not by the command, but by the look in Chloe's eyes and the silence that followed, she eased herself down on the bed.

"I have some bad news. Your psychiatrist, Dr. Richard Fleming, has been murdered. It was in yesterday's paper. He was found in his office still sitting in his chair, gripping his cell phone."

Maggie was numb. "When? Not the day I saw him?"

Chloe nodded. "That evening."

"Oh–no. He didn't deserve that," Maggie moaned. "He was a good man, irritating at times, sure, but, well, you know what I mean. He tried his best to help others–and help me.

"I was such an ass. I saw him as 'the authority,' as if he was trying to trick me or something, and all along it was me playing tricks on him. He saw through it all, Chloe. He knew!"

"Maybe you were playing tricks on yourself, Maggie."

There was a long pause. "Maybe," Maggie said in a whisper.

"By the way, Lena said that you spent nights here out on the front steps, talking. You said you were having conversations with another person, yet she saw no one but you."

Maggie couldn't believe what Chloe was saying. "No! That can't be. No!" She said it defiantly, defending herself. "She saw Curtis the second morning I was here. I told you, she *called* him to take me to the AA meeting. He was leaning at the front desk with his hat in hand as I came out of the stairwell. I waved to him. I remember Lena turning and looking. She *had* to have seen him."

Chloe gave her a quizzical look. "Are you sure it wasn't Kurt she called? Kurt Gunderson?"

This remark stopped Maggie cold. She did recall something Lena had said that morning about Kurt Gunderson saying she had to make her own way to the AA meeting. So perhaps she hadn't called Curtis at all.

Chloe couldn't look her in the eye. She turned away as she murmured, "Perhaps there *was* no Curtis."

Maggie stared toward the door at nothing at all as tears formed in her sad, defeated eyes.

"I think I'll take my meds now."

***

Leaning against the building near the kitchen entrance, the tall shadowy man listened to his boss over the phone:

"Good job. Now finish it up–then off to terminal three for the 9:40 flight on American Airlines. There will be a car waiting for you at your arrival. It won't look like a rental, more like a loaner with dents. The key will be under the floor mat."

"As you say, Doctor." Kurt Gunderson hung up and smiled. He was beginning to love his job, sick as it was. As he was.

***

Chloe stepped out of Maggie's room. She didn't like the job of delivering bad news, especially a murder. It was also her obligation to tell her about her imaginary friend, like it or not.

Maggie really believed there was another person with her out on the front steps. Chloe got goose bumps thinking about it. *Poor thing, she's been through hell.* She slipped behind the front desk to check messages. She retrieved the fax from last night and folded it and tucked into her front pocket. There were no messages. She sat down and checked in with Dr. Mo's office.

CHAPTER EIGHTEEN

7:14 AM

Cutting pieces of duct tape from a roll, the thin, shadowy man stepped out of a room and into the corridor, slinking up toward the main entrance. He stuck a piece of tape to the back of his hand. He paused at the corner to check the front door. All was quiet except for Chloe's voice on the phone. He looked up the hallway to the stairwell.

He edged around the corner near Maggie's room. Looking both ways and seeing no one, he quietly turned the doorknob and slipped in.

Maggie was sobbing on the edge of the bed, wiping tears from her eyes. Her visitor smiled and slowly, silently peeled off the short strip of duct tape from his hand.

With a single step he reached and grabbed her shoulder with one hand. Startled, she pushed back, saying, "Who are you?" and tried to resist, but the other hand holding the duct tape smashed hard across her mouth. She fought but her strength failed her. As she tried to scream, he slugged her hard on the chin, again and again. She heard the bones of her jaw shatter as she fell back on her bed, helpless.

Everything necessary for the job was sitting on the dresser. He glanced at the semi-conscious body on the bed. Taking the carton of milk and the bottles of pills from the dresser, he sat down next to Maggie. He pulled a long-bladed jack-knife from his front pants pocket and flipped it open.

Looking at it, he saw a drop of dried blood on the handle and the blade covered with a sticky crimson residue. He smiled at the memory.

But no time for sentiment. He reached and put the pointed edge to her throat and made a quick, deep jab. Blood rushed and trickled down to the bedspread. He liked that—a dramatic touch. He stood over her, holding the knife to her mouth. With a practiced flick of his wrist, he made two quick slashes.

It was a neat and tidy opening from one side of her face to the other. Her jaw dropped.

Time seemed to stand still for the killer. He liked his work. Taking pills from a bottle, he dropped several in her bleeding mouth and pulled her up next to him. He took the silky white milk and poured it into her blood-filled mouth. She gagged, coughed, and involuntarily swallowed.

He dropped in more pills and milk. It caused gagging noises as she swallowed and gagged again and again. White milk and crimson blood flowed from her mouth. Blood oozed from the jab under her neck.

She was coming to and tried pushing him away. A tremendous pain shot through her head. He pinched her nostrils together and forced more pills down her throat.

I must fight! I have to fight! Maggie rallied again but not for long. Her body went limp. There was no light, no tunnel. *Angels of mercy, take me.* She had one last thought: *William, help my baby.* The darkness soon became nothingness.

He put a finger to her external carotid artery. He felt no pulse. Bottles of morphine, Paxil, Ativan, and Clexa were strewn about the bloody floor.

He folded her body into a fetal position and draped the white bed sheet over her. But he didn't like that. He was proud of his handiwork; why hide it? He yanked the sheet off her body and tossed it aside.

He stood, turning to the mirror, and peered at the reflection of the body on the bed. That's when something strange happened. In the mirror he could see another face far away, staring at him. It zoomed closer, then closer yet.

All of a sudden the face *lurched out of the mirror.* Its mouth opened, and a bright red tongue jutted forth. On it were tiny white maggots.

Hundreds of the little white devils leaped from the mouth. More maggots followed. In a flash, Kurt Gunderson was covered head to toe with the tiny white slithering things. They were inside his clothes, crawling over his bare skin–thousands of them.

Covered with the crawling larvae, he could no longer see himself in the mirror. Screaming, he panicked as he dashed for the door, running and stumbling along the hallway, brushing and slapping at the maggots on his face and neck. Through the dining hall and out the kitchen door, he ran all the way to his car.

***

Chloe was on the phone, setting up appointments with Dr. Mo's patients, when she heard the commotion. She ran, following the noise along the hallway and corridor, to the kitchen.

Running fast, slipping and falling, she got to her feet and kept running until she was inside the kitchen. She found nothing, though her elbow hurt like hell. She looked at it. It wasn't bleeding, but there were tiny white things on it. *Maggots?* She hated bugs period, but maggots were the worst. *How did they get here?* She shuddered as she flicked them off her skin with her other hand.

She looked around. All was quiet. Then suddenly she heard the squealing of tires and saw a cloud of dust as a car peeled off down the back entrance heading out to the highway.

As she rested her hand on the wall near the kitchen entrance, her right foot slowly slid on the marble floor. She lifted her white nurse shoe. Several squashed white maggots wiggled; some were flattened while others oozed grey matter. Panic filled her throat and lungs. She stomped a shoe to the floor again and again.

Chloe took her hand off the wall. There was a maggot on her palm. She brushed it off and wiped her hands on her skirt. She gasped for air as she turned to head back up the maggot-filled hallway. The tiny white larvae were scattered everywhere.

She charged to Maggie's room. The doors she passed along the corridor seemed never-ending, as if she were moving in slow motion.

Her shoes slid over the tiny, squirming maggots but she kept her balance. She couldn't run fast enough. Finally, she rounded the corner and dashed into Maggie's room.

She was naked, curled up in a fetal position. On the floor Chloe saw the spilt milk, blood, empty bottles of pills, and more maggots.

"No. This can't be! Maggie," she yelled, "Maggie! Wake up." She bent to shake her. It was then that she saw the duct tape and blood oozing around the corners of her mouth, and the puncture wound under her chin. Screaming, she ran down the hall to the phone and punched in 911.

Back in Maggie's room, Chloe flashed through her ABC's. She checked her airways. Nothing in her throat. Then she pressed her carotid—no pulse. Quickly she climbed on the bed and began CPR with mouth-to-mouth resuscitation. There was no response. She moved to chest compressions.

She pushed hard and often, then back to mouth-to-mouth, and back to chest compressions. Chloe's strokes were smooth and direct with rhythmic precision.

Sirens wailed far away, becoming louder and closer as Chloe kept at it, using her skills to the best of her ability. Like Maggie, she wasn't a quitter.

When the EMTs arrived, they had to pull her off her patient. One attended to Chloe out in the hallway as the other two shoved a tube far down Maggie's throat to her stomach and pumped it out. They too, practiced their profession the best they knew how, for time was critical and time was of the essence.

***

Chloe gasped. She caught her breath, and with a brush of her arm, pushed the smelling salts away and sat up. She ran her hands through her hair and listened to the EMTs back in Maggie's room. She didn't like the tone. From the sound of it, the sense of urgency was gone, though they hadn't stopped their efforts to get the patient breathing again.

Another emergency vehicle pulled up outside and two paramedics wheeled in a gurney. Dr. Morris Gallagher followed the vehicle from his office. He ran ahead of them stopping at the front desk where Chloe was sitting, catching her breath and dabbing her reddened eyes.

The look between the two said it all. He walked fast and entered the patient's room observing, thinking for a moment, and then frowning. He checked her vitals, instructed the EMT'S, and stepped back out of the room.

CHAPTER NINETEEN

7:36 AM

From the backseat of the Ford Taurus, Mickey spoke. "You haven't been back in that building since December, 1949. Got any feelings about that?"

"Bones. Digging up bones—again," was all Gordon could think of, and that was his reply.

"Uh-oh," Mickey murmured, spotting the flashing and rotating red lights on the emergency vehicles. Kat grabbed Gordon's wrist. M.G. and Mickey exchanged worried looks.

He pulled around the two florescent yellow vehicles and drove up and over the curb, onto the grassy terrace next to the building. They bolted from the car and raced inside to the front desk.

Gordon said, "We're here to see Maggie."

Dr. Gallagher nodded to the newcomers, then turned to his nurse. "It's time, Chloe," he said as he headed back up to the room. The others followed.

He watched the EMTs do what they had been trained to do. Without skipping a beat or interrupting them he put on his stethoscope and set the chest piece on Maggie's chest. The oxygen mask had been placed over her mouth and nose. There was no heartbeat—none that he could detect, anyway.

"It doesn't look good, huh?" Mickey didn't know what else to say.

Gordon's eyes rolled when he heard sirens approaching outside. "Brilliant." He glanced wearily over his shoulder as two squad cars pulled up out front.

Dr. Gallagher stepped out of the way of the EMTs as they continued fast, rhythmic pushes to her chest. He walked back to the group as Chloe introduced herself to them.

He greeted the officers in blue. "You'd better take a look. The EMTs are still at it, but they're preparing to take her to Lutheran Medical. She hasn't been breathing for at least twenty minutes, probably longer. I did all I could do."

The woman officer took her hat off, revealing streaked dishwater blonde hair. "Foul play?"

"She's got a broken jaw. They're having a hell of a time keeping the oxygen mask on her."

The woman officer nodded. "How many people are in this building? And how many had access to the patient?"

Chloe stepped up next to the doctor. "There were only two people in this building this morning, ma'am. Just me and her." Her hands were trembling. Both officers took note.

"No one else?" she asked. Silence. "I said, no one else here? Speak up!" She was in command, at least in her own mind.

Chloe answered her just to shut her up. "I didn't see anyone. Only heard a commotion coming from the corridor that leads to the kitchen."

Mickey left the others to investigate the corridor and kitchen area, as well as outside the back of the building.

"Just you and the patient?" The female cop kept it up, hoping for a more plausible answer.

Chloe frowned and answered again. "Well, yes, I wasn't supposed to be here but Lena, who practically runs this place, left a message, uh, voice mail at Dr. Mo's office early this morning, around one-thirty I think.

"She sounded out of breath. She said there was an emergency and had to visit an ailing cousin. I work out of Dr. Morris Gallagher's office, and as a visiting nurse, took over for her. I've been called here from time to time."

The female officer asked, "So, you're saying that no one has seen this, uh, Lena, for a day or so?"

"Only Maggie would know the answer to that." Chloe responded with a sigh.

The EMTs wheeled Maggie out of her room and past the group gathered around the front desk. One arm had dropped, dangling off the side of the cot as it was being wheeled down the steps and into the back of the ambulance. There was no attempt to restrain it.

The officer spoke again. "In a few minutes our back-up will be here to take statements from all of you. Stick around."

***

Mickey briskly walked around the corner to the group. He was cupping his hands.

"What'd you find, Mick?" Gordon asked.

"Just these," he said, opening his hands.

"Oh, *Gawd.*" Kat grimaced and put a hand to her throat to keep from gagging. "I need to sit down."

Chloe said, "If any of you want to follow me to the chapel, we can sit, meditate, and talk this out." She shifted her eyes to the female officer.

"Thanks for the offer, hon, but we'll stay out here until our back-up arrives."

The others followed Chloe down the hall. They passed two doors on the right, stopping at the first door on the left with a brushed metal sign on it that read, Chapel. They stopped and waited.

Mickey sped around the corner, wiping his hands as he tried to catch up with the others. Once there, Chloe opened the door.

Dr. Gallagher was the first to go in. The room was dark except for a dimly lit floor lamp off to the side of the altar, next to the lectern. It gave a soft, almost eerie yellow-green glow.

He glanced at the three rows of pews and motioned for the others to make themselves comfortable. They entered, heads lowered in reverence, one at a time marching to the back pew, except for M.G. She stepped in, turned toward the front, and kept walking.

The others saw it too. There was a collective gasp. "There!" she said, pointing toward the altar. Gordon quickly stepped out of the chapel and summoned the officers.

***

"So Lena never left this place," Chloe murmured as tears filled her eyes.

M.G. pushed her hands outward palms up as she walked the length of Lena's final resting place. Her ashen, plump legs were bent at the knees and hung over the end of the altar. She was wearing a pleated maroon skirt with a white blouse. Around her neck was a sterling silver chain and a crystal-studded silver cross, and simple wedding band alluding to her symbolic marriage to Jesus, who had saved her.

M.G. circled the body twice, whispering in a chant-like monotone: "You have permission to leave, Lena. Go to the Light. It calls your name. Unconditional love awaits you. Go, Lena! Jesus is waiting for you with outstretched arms to hold you forevermore."

***

"Anybody have a clue about the writing on the duct tape over her mouth?" the male officer asked.

The dull silver-colored tape looked the same as the strip on Maggie's mouth, Dr. Gallagher recalled. "Obviously, the same guy did this."

Written in red were the letters FLOC. No one said a word. Kat stepped back to the first pew and sat down next to Chloe, folding her hands in prayer.

The others surrounded the body on the altar. Mickey was in deep thought as he glanced to Gordon, then looked away.

"FLOC. Got anything?" Gordon peered into his old partner's eyes. "We both know that LOC stood for the Legionnaires of Christ or Cristo all those years ago. *And* that it still exists in one form or another, however culturally and integrated it may have become. The ideology lives on."

"Yeah," Mickey replied. "It could have morphed, or it's an offshoot group. One thing, though. Back then it had to do with the buying and selling of children. If it's connected with Fleming, Maggie, and this woman, where's that connection?"

Gordon was stumped. "None I can think of."

Mickey's eyes widened. "Wait a sec. When I called the FBI in Phoenix, they told me that FLOC was written on Fleming too." Mickey rubbed his chin.

"Yeah?" Gordon's mind was in top gear, working fast.

The police motioned for Dr. Gallagher to examine the body. The others gathered near the last pew. Kat and Chloe prayed while Gordon, Mickey, and M.G. conversed in low voices.

"I'd say she's been dead five or six hours," Dr. Gallagher said. "It's just a guess, though."

Talking quietly, Gordon whispered, "Whoever the killer is, he's efficient." Changing his thoughts, he turned to his old pal. "Okay, Mick, we know what the initials LOC stand for, but what's with the F?"

"Fuck—I mean," Mickey stammered, "I have a hunch. I'm thinking it through. That trail of maggots led all the way down the hall here and through the kitchen and outside. Obviously the killer had a vehicle and knew his way around here. The bugs, they were on the floor where Margaret was, too. By the way, Gordy, the kitchen looks the same as it did when you and I were there."

"Visit the wine cellar too?" Gordon asked.

"Didn't get that far yet," Mickey responded, "but the maggots ... I say we follow the maggots and we find the killer. Maybe more."

"The autopsy should prove me right," Dr. Gallagher said. "Strangled from behind. Other than the duct tape and small puncture wound under the chin, there's not a mark on her. Chloe, the officers out in the hallway want a word with you."

***

"Yes sir, like I said, just me and the resident here, Maggie. And ... uh, who am I talking to?" Chloe asked.

"Excuse us, Ma'am. I'm officer Lord, Gene Lord. My partner here is Bobbie. Officer Bobbie Swinehart."

"Thank you," Chloe said and proceeded to answer the question. "Yes, there's a janitor here. A shady character, no one ever seems to see him. He's around but only Lena knows what he does and where he lives, and she's–"

"Then he must be on file here somewhere." Officer Lord interrupted. "We'll check the Rolodex and file cabinets if you don't mind, ma'am."

Chloe nodded. "I'd like to know more about him myself."

The group was ushered out of the chapel by Officer Swinehart. They brainstormed in the hallway.

"We've got plenty of questions, that's for sure," Dr. Gallagher said. "Is there someplace where we could talk this through?"

CHAPTER TWENTY

7:59 AM - The Kitchen

"Three murders—one in Phoenix, two here. Maggie knew the other two personally. The others knew her, though separately." As Mickey spoke, his mind was in his mental file section, trying to tie everything together. "Oh, yeah. FLOC was sliced into Dr. Fleming's forehead. That's what I forgot. Not to mention the small incision under his chin near his trachea, like the others here."

They sat at one of the round tables in the dining hall, except for Gordon, who paced the room restlessly. Mick and the others shot him a glance before he spoke.

"We don't have time to fart around, guys. We've got three murders in three days! There's a big piece of the puzzle missing and it's got to be right here in this building someplace. Mick, you say Margaret knew the other two. Then I say we start with her situation first. Agreed?"

The group talked it out around the wooden table and nodded their assent to Gordon.

"We gotta work fast," he said. "Kat, go with M.G. and Chloe. Go through all of Maggie's belongings. Check everything. If she has a computer, hack it if you can. Get her emails, cell phone, anything that might help us."

The women headed for the door. Chloe called after them: "Maggie journaled. You won't find it in there, though. Her original room is on the third floor, first door on your right. Her name's still on the door."

Turning back to the table, she continued, "Maybe you and Mickey could explore up there, too. Could be something there."

"Right. I'll look into that," Gordon responded.

They stopped at the doorway and paused. M.G. went in first and said, "Try not to step on the little whities. They're all over the floor. I've been doing long-distance Reiki on her computer. I've asked Spirit to allow me to access her computer. Check under the bed."

"Uh, this is not my field of expertise, folks," Dr. Gallagher said. "I'm sorry for your loss. She was a tough cookie. If you'll excuse me, I should get back to my office."

They stood still for a moment after he left, staring at the little wooden door that led to the wine cellar.

"Go ahead, Mick, take a gander. I'm going up to the third floor to look around."

"Stopping on the second to see your old room?" Mick asked.

Gordon paused before speaking. "I'm not going down that road again."

Up the staircase he went. Stopping on the second landing, he looked at the door. He touched the cold doorknob. *Fuck it.*

He climbed the final step, pushed the door open and walked the third floor hallway, stopping at the first door on the right. Maggie's welcome card was still there.

The memories came flooding back to the former sheriff of Pine Nut. It was in this building that he was a high school freshman; it was a different place now. At the time, it was a building holding dark secrets--secrets so ugly that life became a living nightmare for him.

The door was ajar. He eased it open with the back of his hand all the way. It was dark. He stepped in and opened the blinds, including the south window in the corner. As he stood near that south window he looked the room over as if trying to recollect the past.

He took a couple of steps toward the cot at the other end of the room and stopped. Reaching into his pocket, he pulled out a pen-light and got down on his knees. The god-awful memories returned unbidden. Sweat formed on his brow and forehead. His palms became clammy, but he had a job to do.

He bent down and peered under the bed. Moving the empty chamber pot out of the way, he shined his penlight on the baseboard. *I'll be damned,* he thought, *it's still there.*

Images of his past, the twisted rituals, came crashing back. Gordon revisited them only briefly before desperately breaking free. He shook away those thoughts as he focused on the baseboard. It was still there, the writings of two frightened kids.

***

"I'm in, ladies. AOL, Yahoo, Gmail, what?"

"Do your Reiki, girl," Kat said.

M.G. scanned AOL as Kat and Chloe leaned in behind her. "Nothing here. My gut says Gmail.

"What's the name of her daughter?" M.G. asked.

"Bliss," Chloe shot back. "They weren't on speaking terms, though. Maggie had been trying for months to contact her. She heard nothing. She was all torn up about it. It ate at her that she couldn't make peace with her daughter before she—"

"Bingo, I'm in! Look, in the subject headings," M.G. blurted as she pointed. "HELP ME MOM."

Mickey came bounding into the room as the three women huddled around the laptop.

"Get Gordon! He needs to see this," Kat said. Mickey stiffened and then raced to the stairwell and took a bounce to the first step just as Gordon reached the bottom of it. They collided. "Goddamn it, Mick! Why do you always do that to me?"

"They got something. Follow me," Mickey said.

"You scared the hell out of me, you know," Gordon muttered. Climbing up and down three flights of stairs had already winded him, and getting spooked by Mickey on top of it was not the best thing for his old, damaged heart.

Mick said half-angrily, "We got shit to do and fast. I'm getting my laptop out of the car. We'll go over the files, including the one on Aaron Betz."

When he returned with his laptop, the women were setting up Maggie's laptop on the front desk counter. "We can breathe easier here," Chloe said, and Kat, Mickey and Gordon nodded in understanding.

"Okay, let's open her email," M.G. said as she tapped the mouse area on Maggie's laptop. Chloe, Kat, Gordon, and Mickey all leaned in.

Gotta be quick—am in a lava tube here in Hawaii. There's armed guards—a dozen or so—other girls here too, pregnant. We are chained--Old man here seems to know you—he's in charge—had a face-lift—baby, factory...

"What the hell–?" Mickey said.

Gordon turned to Chloe and said, "Go to the hospital and stay with the body."

"Why?" she asked.

"I'm listening to the little voices again," he said.

Mickey shook his head.

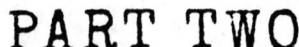

PART TWO

CHAPTER TWENTY-ONE

August 13 9:41 AM

C hloe ran out swinging her arms and fists. "Get away from her, you incompetent bastards!" She connected several times, knocking one orderly to the ground.

She was standing just inside the emergency room entrance of Capital City Lutheran Hospital. It was there that she heard the stretcher tip and hit the concrete as they pulled it out of the back of the ambulance. She turned in horror as Maggie's body hit the cement, face-first. Her head bounced.

Enraged, Chloe shouted at the EMTs, "You cocksuckers! How could you be so inept, so clumsy, so *stupid* as to drop her body on the concrete floor?" She screamed. *"You fucking, incredibly stupid bastards!"*

It took some time before the three EMTs could wrestle her to the ground. When they finally had her arms and legs pinned down, one of them gave her a hypo, but not before she expended all of her considerable strength and wrath. The three were bloody and hurting.

Once back to her senses, she stayed close to Margaret. Outside the cold room, Chloe sat on a folding chair guarding the lone body in the hospital morgue. On occasion she would step inside, rub her cold, clammy arms, and talk to her as if she were still alive. She continued telling the lifeless body about her life, her childhood, her parents, and the emptiness she felt at that moment.

Chloe's mind reeled through a sad, hazy mist. What more could she do? With a patient at her side, she was a good nurse. Alone, she could only cry.

***

"Mick, you actually spotted a maggot on the floor at a busy airport, at your age?" Gordon knew that he pumped his buddy's ego about a hundred and fifty percent.

Tapping his temple with his right index finger, Mick leaned with a wry grin, saying, "Still got it, boss. Did you see anyone suspicious get on this plane?"

"Nope," Gordon said as he shook his head. "The only guy who looked out of place was helping an old lady down the ramp. He's sitting next to her in the back. My guess, though, is that the perp jumped the first flight out of here. I would have. By the way, did you find anything of interest in the wine cellar?"

Mick shrugged. "Someone's using it as a half-assed office. The old wine kegs are gone. Has a new floor, a cot, and a flimsy desk down there with a radio and an HP desktop. I told the cops, so they'll be dusting for prints, scoping it out. The usual shit."

They sat in the second row. The plane idled on the Capital City Airport runway with its jet engines purring behind two others waiting for takeoff.

Gordon held the sheet of paper that Chloe had pulled off the fax machine at Evergreen Meadows. It was blank, except for the telephone number at the top edge of the paper, showing its origin. Why? He flicked his wrist, holding the paper to Mickey. "Why send a blank fax? A signal, maybe?"

"Had to be," Mickey agreed, adding, "but he failed. Whoever it was meant for didn't get rid of it. Or didn't have time to."

"Agreed," Gordon said. "If I'm not mistaken it was sent from–"

"Area code 480," Mickey said, "Fleming's office!" He scanned his new iPhone for numbers. "Yup. His machine. Whoever killed Fleming either came here to carry on, or, as you say, sent a message to someone here to–continue the killing?"

Gordon said, "Either Margaret was on to something, or someone was keeping tabs on her."

"Bingo, boss. Keeping tabs on her *and* Fleming. As if they, whoever 'they' are, were about to be exposed."

Gordon took it in and said, "I'll agree for the time being, Mick. So ... what'd you learn about Betz?"

They were interrupted by the sound and fury of the ATR 72 gunning its engines, starting ever so slowly before rapidly gaining speed. The nose pointed upward as it lifted off the runway, screaming toward Dallas. They sat heavy in their adjoining seats, pushed back by the g-force of the roaring engines.

Rubbing his hand across the day-old stubble under his chin and cheeks and thinking about taking his nitro-glycerin tablets, Gordon sighed, "I'm getting too old for this crap."

"Oh, horseshit, Gordy," Mickey retorted. "You ain't old. Old is what happens on the day you die. You can't get any older."

"About Aaron Betz," Mickey said. "Scanned a few info sites. FBI, CIA, like that. He got himself a fake diploma from the University of Iowa, though I doubt he ever set foot in the state. If he did, I'd hope that he would have stepped in cowshit up to his knees.

"Anyway, I found three birth certificates. The sonofabitch has been up to no good for quite some time. Maybe the reason he was booted out of the CIA in less than three weeks. Entered a Jesuit seminary in LaCrosse, Wisconsin, just across the Mississippi River from Minnesota. No record of him becoming a priest, however.

"Enrolled in a medical school in Boston. Again no record of a certificate, graduation, or diploma. A several year span between the seminary and med school in Boston. Few years younger than you, I'm guessing.

"Seems he got younger with each birth certificate. Sketchy bastard, ain't he?"

"Yeah. Sketchy," Gordon said, thinking of Bliss's email. "Name changes. Body-face-altering? Sounds like our old friend Larry."

Mickey agreed, Yeah, he got off the hook back in '49, '53, and '67, like a cat with nine lives, the sly bastard. He's the one . . . ain't he?"

"He's always been the one," Gordon said.

Mickey replied. "You know there's a connection here, don't you? And then there's Bliss."

Gordon pondered their situation as he pulled on the sagging chicken skin below his first chin. He never liked looking into the mirror and seeing it. He always thought of having it removed. Justifying the cost of it had kept him from having it done.

Yes, Betz was the one and the same murderous bastard that they'd been chasing ever since they became partners. It's the reason he and Mick were drawn back to the beginning.

They weren't getting any younger. This would be the last caper for the former sheriff. As for the Mick, you just never know. They had to come back for Maggie and for their old friend Richard Fleming. And because Richard had gotten it right.

More importantly, they had to do it for themselves. Mick was there for his buddy. Yes, he was there for himself, too. The Mick had never let a case go unsolved before.

This one evil fuck-up was a peculiar breed. Each time they caught up with the bastard, he'd find a way to slip away and get lost, and stay lost for years at a time. But this particular caper was like no other.

Lawrence Burke was *the* great puzzle for Mickey Zaugbaum. It altered his life from the get-go. It's why he stayed in the field of crime fighting and espionage. The only criminal he had yet to nab bothered him something fierce. He didn't like things that go bump in the night, either. And this case was like that–bumpy.

And then there was Gordon. He had a cross to bear and it was getting heavy. There would be no turning back, no surrenders, no negotiations–not this time.

"We change planes in Dallas, Mick said, jolting Gordon back from his daydream. "Then it's on to Waikiki, the Big Island, and the final chapter, old man."

Gordon grunted. "I want to find Maggie's Bliss and get the crazy bastard we've been chasing for the past fifty years, or die trying."

CHAPTER TWENTY-TWO

10:09 AM

Mickey Zaugbaum was spry and ten years Gordon's junior. He didn't like the way his mentor talked. It wasn't like him. Laid back, yes, a country boy at heart, yes, always had a great mind for solving crimes–all yes. But a quitter?

If Gordon Maxwell sucked at anything, it was crossword puzzles. Used a pocket dictionary, even for the easy ones. Gordon never quit trying, though. As they talked he worked the airline's magazine puzzle. When he thought Mick wasn't looking, he'd flip to the back pages and look at the completed version. He couldn't concentrate.

His mind wandered back, not to Evergreen Meadows, but to the Capital City minor seminary. The same building, yes, but decades earlier it was Gordon's home for one nine-month span. He left home to be away from home, away from his old man, anyway. Gordon's father was a religiously strict, mean sonofabitch, who never thought twice about smacking his only son, his adopted son.

He would hit Gordon fast, in the middle of a conversation, in the middle of a sentence, and he usually hit him with the back of the hand to the face.

That's how Gordon had his eardrums punctured. Too many slaps to the side of the head.

And as for his mother, let's just say that whatever the hell the woman was good at, she sucked the bag as a mother.

The plane leveled off. Gordon sat in the aisle seat and unfastened his seatbelt.

He stepped toward the back, teetering along the way, touching the top of a seat now and then to keep from staggering. Breathing hard, he scoped out the passengers along the way, but found no one looking nervous or out of place. Then again, a cold-blooded killer isn't the nervous type.

Reaching the back of the plane, he had two rows to pass before stepping into the lavatory. The last seat to his right held a nondescript man with a mustache in his late thirties-early forties and a short older woman. The man in the aisle seat was scrunched around as best he could in the tight, limited space. With a small pillow on his lap, he had his head on the shoulder the elderly woman with his eyes closed. She looked up at Gordon with a tired smile as he passed by.

Once inside the tight quarters he stood and leaned on the edge of the small sink and grimaced. The lavatory had that same old smell. No matter how many plane rides he had taken over the years, that airplane smell never changed.

Looking into the mirror, he grabbed a tissue from the wall dispenser and wiped the cold sweat from his forehead.

He reached into the side pocket of his light brown, elbow-patched sport coat and took out a small bottle. He fumbled with the lid.

Goddamn childproof lids. It's easier for a four-year-old to shoot a fucking revolver than pry off these plastic safety caps. The pharmaceutical companies ought to be shot. He shook out a nitro tab and placed under his tongue. He sat on the commode until he felt better.

Turning the latch and opening the door, he stepped out to find a lady waiting in the aisle with her legs tightly pressed together. No smile. The other lavatory was occupied. He stepped past her on his way up to the front. Glancing to his left, he noticed the aisle seat was vacant. The old woman had a blanket up to her chin and her head rested on the windowless wall.

Steadier now, he made his way to his seat and friends with ease. Something haunted him. He had that old feeling that something was amiss. Back in the day he had time and resources to figure it out, the old gut instinct for instance. Now, he wasn't so sure that he had it any more. He did have his wife, his old friend and partner, Mick, and M.G., a woman he hardly knew, but, like Mick, she sure knew her business. It was time to talk.

The discussion started with their arrival at Evergreen Meadows. Dr. Richard Fleming had arranged it. Was this his last act as a good psychiatrist, as a man of healing? His one last chance to help his last patient, Margaret Lynne Hornsby? Maybe. Perhaps he knew something else, yet he couldn't put a finger on it, so he had his close friends help him solve the last two items on his agenda: curing his patient and finding his killers. Perhaps. Perhaps, indeed.

The talks centered around Maggie's' murder, the untimely demise of the nun, Lena Lundy, the whereabouts of the character named Kurt Gunderson, and the recent departure of Dr. Aaron Betz. Why did he leave a note for his nurse, M.G., stating that he was abruptly leaving town, with or without an explanation? Betz had to be Burke. Or was he? Then there was the visiting nurse, Chloe.

For the next hour and a half, Gordon and Mickey retraced the course of events that had brought them to this point.

The plane landed in Dallas. Kat and M.G. took a position across the wide walkway near the ladies room and leaned against the wall. From their vantage point they could scan the sitting area and walkway as well as exiting passengers.

Gordon and Mickey stood off to the window side of the gate, as close to the exiting group as possible, yet back and out of sight of those disembarking. They counted the passengers.

"Sixty-three passengers including themselves," Mickey reported. "One's missing. There were seventy-eight seats but only sixty-four passengers. I didn't see that man or the old lady, Gordon. I noticed an older guy with mustache and goatee, wearing baggy clothing and a fedora. Didn't see him get on back in Capital City, did you?"

Gordon scratched his head. "The guy with the stooped shoulders and walked funny?"

"But that guy didn't have any facial hair, Gordy."

CHAPTER TWENTY-THREE

12:55 PM - Dallas/Fort Worth

G ordon said, "I'll go back on the plane and check on the old lady. You tip off the women. Check the men's rooms and try not to get arrested like that Idaho senator."

Gordon talked his way back onto the plane. The flight crew and attendants were gathered in the back.

There was commotion behind him and someone said, "Please, sir, step out of the way." Gordon ducked and slipped into a row of seats as paramedics trotted to the back with their equipment.

He watched the futile attempt to revive the woman. It bothered him more than any of them could ever know. He didn't want this or any part of it. It was becoming an emotional drain. He was breathing heavily again and there were pains in his chest.

Why did I make this trip?

He didn't have to answer the question that haunted him; he already knew the answer. Kat had tried talking him out of going back to Capital City. Yet she knew he had to go. Without her he'd be like a kite in the wind, with no one holding the string. He needed her. Kat was his rock, his wife, and his lover. He couldn't live without her. Not long, anyway.

Those eerie feelings were back. Something was terribly wrong. Innocent ones were dying. This whole thing ate at him like hyenas feasting on the decaying remains of an impala. He couldn't stop it.

***

Time slowed to a crawl back in the security office. The four sat on plastic chairs waiting for the opportunity to speak. Gordon was pissed. "These pricks are so fucking into themselves and protocol," he whispered to Mick, "by the time we get to explain what and who they should be looking for, he'll be long gone."

"Security? Security for who?" M.G. asked the female security officer. "We aren't allowed to speak unless spoken to for our security? No wonder there's a border problem with illegals. *They've* got no problem, *we've* got the problem!"

The stocky woman with the badge said, "Cool it, lady. You're startin' to be drag." She spoke like she'd just swallowed a bug.

"Cool nothin'!" M.G. was on a roll. "You guys couldn't catch a mouse with a handful of cheese and a hungry cat. Listen, it's a matter of life and death. You guys aren't asking any questions!

"There's a trail of dead people from Arizona to Indiana and now to Texas. What the hell is going on here? At least look for a puncture wound under her chin. Couldn't you do *that*, for chrissake?"

The oldest, overweight male security officer adjusted his gun belt and leaned against the door with the usual authoritative smirk. M.G. pissed him off, too. He had little time for women, especially an intelligent woman with a fast mouth.

He took a bite from his ham sandwich. Without fully chewing it, he said, "Until the Dallas police arrive, we own you. Just sit tight and shut your filthy mouth.

"We got a dead passenger on our hands here and you four are interested in her. Well, boys and girls, we're interested in *you*. You see, we don't trust you, your I.D.s, *or* your story. The three of us don't even *like* you guys. Don't like your attitude. Your *accents,* y'all speak Northern!

"We got the guns and badges," he went on, mayonnaise leaking from his lips, "we got control here. And we got you!" The pompous ass took another bite of his sandwich as a piece of iceberg lettuce fell from his mouth to the floor. He kicked it aside.

The two subordinate officers chuckled appreciatively at their cohort's performance, as if they were in on something no one else knew about. They were wrong.

There was a tap on the glass-paneled door. Mickey stood. He had phoned an acquaintance earlier while waiting. The guard in charge set his half-eaten sandwich on the edge of the desk. It fell off and landed in the wastepaper basket as he stepped out, closing the door behind him.

Outside the room a trim, middle-aged man in a blue business suit produced a thin wallet. He flipped it open and the guard's eyes widened. He became slack-jawed with embarrassment as the middle-aged man opened the door and said to the two security guards inside the room, "If you two will excuse us, we have business to conduct. You'll have to wait outside with your friend." The smirks were gone, replaced with reddened faces as the guards cleared out of the room.

"What's the skinny, guys?" the Dallas FBI director asked.

Forty minutes later they were high over Albuquerque, headed for an island paradise.

The Boeing 777 with twin Rolls Royce Trent 892 engines, purred like a lapful of kittens. The plush seats swiveled. The former airport captives faced each other as they conversed. It was all new to them-first class, that is. Mickey's FBI friend had arranged it.

M.G. sat next to Kat. She had a question. "Back in the kitchen at Evergreen Meadows, I noticed that you weren't fully engaged in our conversation. Any reason?"

Kat blushed as she pushed on the armrests, getting more comfortable. "Nothing to do with you. It was that place, M.G."

"Sorry I brought it up," M.G. said, poking nervously at her cell phone.

"Don't be," Kat said. "It was a turning point in my life and Gordon's. We married a few months later. Second marriage for both of us."

"And your story?" Kat asked.

M.G. reached into her small purse and pulled out a two-ouncer. Flashing her hand at the attendant passing by, she asked if she could have a Coke.

The middle-aged male flight attendant peered down at her and frowned. "No Coke. Pepsi."

M.G. nodded briefly, crinkling her nose without looking up. She turned to Kat as he light-footed it to the galley for a Pepsi. "Can't they be a little younger, nicer?"

Kat shook her head. "Gordon is still mourning the sixties. You know, back when the flight attendants were called 'stewardesses' and they were all under thirty and wore miniskirts. It was a man's world then. I suppose they're as disappointed as we are."

"A point well taken," M.G. agreed.

"I should write a letter to that minister's wife. You know, the one who got bitchy with the attendant a few years ago, and say, 'I empathize with you.' Naw. She doesn't like anyone that looks different than her. White. Blonde, thin, with religious and political views to the right of Attila the Hun."

She added the two-ounce bourbon to her Pepsi once it arrived, and raised her glass. *"Salut."* She downed it before setting it back on her tray.

Wiping the corners of her mouth, M.G. said, "So you want my story, huh?"

Before Kat could answer, M.G. raised a "wait" finger and turned to Mickey, who appeared engrossed in Margaret's laptop. "Any response from her? How many emails did you send to Bliss back in Dallas?"

"Three," he replied. "Told her that we were on our way and to hang tough, before we left Dallas. I'll let you know if she replied after we land."

M.G. nodded and turned back to Kat. "Where was I? Okay, the beginning. What can I say? Surviving my childhood wasn't easy. I spent time in juvenile corrections, twice. It shaped my thoughts, shall we say."

Kat frowned, saying, "Sorry I brought it up."

"No, it's just that to answer why or how I got involved with chasing sickos, there's no short answer. Then again, we have an eight-hour flight."

"Great," said Kat, "so give me the blow-by-blow."

M.G. sank back into her plush swivel-seat. "I had one parent, no sibs. I wrote a poem for Father's Day once. It went something like this...." And she recited from memory:

"TO THE WORLDS GREATEST DAD -
JUST THOUGHT I'D REMIND YOU WHAT YOU MEAN
TO ME.
I KNOW THE TABLE IS ALWAYS SET FOR TWO,
JUST ME AND YOU;
SOME TABLES HAVE SETTINGS FOR THREE:
MOMS, DADDIES, AND KIDS LIKE ME,
AND THAT'S OKAY
ON THIS - FATHERS DAY
AND I LOVE YOU NOW AND ALWAYS -
IS THAT OKAY?
'CAUSE YOU'RE THE ONE WHO TOOK THE TIME TO
RAISE AND
FEED ME AND PUT THE BAND-AIDS ON MY KNEE.
SO IT'S OKAY FOR YOU TO JUST HAVE ME.
I LOVE YOU ON THIS - FATHERS DAY
AND THAT'S ALL I HAVE TO SAY, 'CEPT
YOU ARE THE ONLY PARENT I EVER HAD.
SO FOR A KID LIKE ME, MOM,
YOU ARE THE WORLDS GREATEST DAD!"

Kat clapped her hands in delight. "I love it!"

"Thanks," M.G. said, stone-faced. "My old man left home one day. They argued a lot. One night he beat the living hell out of my mom. I tried to intervene. He slammed me up against a wall and that's the last I remember about that night except for one thing...."

Kat winced. She appeared afraid to ask, to hear the answer, but she felt compelled to ask anyway. "What's the one thing?"

"He picked me up and took me to the back porch. It was there that he sodomized his five-year-old-daughter.

"My mother knew. The next day I was bleeding and had trouble walking. I remember that. She took me to the doctor's office. She swore she'd kill him if he ever stepped foot in the house again. No one knows what happened to him. He never returned. It was as if he just disappeared."

Kat said, "But you survived. Do you feel that you have transcended?"

"Transcended? That means to rise above, become a better person and all that. I am my mother's child, Kat. I walk in her footsteps. There's a dark side to me. Sometimes I like what I do."

***

Gordon shot a look at Mick as he examined the info on Maggie's PC. "Found something about Bliss," Mick said. "You may already know this, but she's a former Marine. Was in the Corps for nine years, so she's no wuss."

Gordon nodded.

"So," Mickey went on, "it appears that Bliss is being held captive somewhere inside an expansive series of lava tubes.

"If several people are being held and there are guards as she says, it's got to be big enough to work in, bring others in and out, go to, leave from, and do all that undetected. Maybe more than one entrance.

"I researched the lava tubes. They were formed thousands of years ago when the volcanoes first erupted, forcing the hot lava to flow into the sea. The crusty tops break through here and there, leaving cave-like openings. What do you think?"

"Gee, Mick," Gordon said sarcastically, "ain't the information age a kick in the head?"

"Bite me, asshole."

"She's on the Big Island, you think?" Gordon asked.

Mick nodded. "The Kilauea volcano has been spewing out lava since 1983 or so. One problem though. If, and I say *if*, we're correct and she *is* on the Big Island, there's hundreds of miles of lava tubes."

"Then I guess we're going spelunking," Gordon replied with a weary sigh.

***

"Yes Kurt. They would be coming here. I know. I know they act dumb. Yes, they're old. Old and dumb like a fox, as the old saying goes. But nothing must interfere now. Find them as soon as you can. Dispose of them wherever you can. Keep me abreast of their whereabouts at all times. Abreast? Abreast means keep me informed, Kurt."

Aaron slammed the handset down, crushing it, pinching his skin. He wasn't happy. The news from Kurt was disconcerting. Examining his hand, he saw a trickle of blood on his palm. Puzzled, he glanced down. He broke the handset, but that's not what concerned him. His right hand was trembling. Again.

"I'm advancing the cause of the FLOC, and *no one shall interfere with my work!*"

CHAPTER TWENTY-FOUR

10:56 AM Hawaii Time

"**H**ey, big Samoan. Want some moa? Unh-unh. You know the rules. You aren't supposed to touch us, remember? Might become attached and lose your focus. Isn't that what the big *kahuna* tells you? Besides, you want a baby—doll and I'm not your type." Bliss didn't smile. She was toying with her captor–again.

"I'll set you free again," he grunted, hoping for a closer encounter with his captive.

Lawai'a copped a feel the first time. She let him. "I know you'd like to walk about. Feel good, like a bitch should, ya."

He talked Island Pidgin as did the others. Working the pineapple fields, there were Filipinos, Japanese, Chinese, Portuguese, you name it, and they were there, working for the man, Dole. They made their own language. Had to, so they could understand each other.

"You be good to me, I be good to you, get it, girl?"

"Um, Lawai'a? That's your name, correct?"

"Oh, ya, sistah. In Hawaiian, it means fisherman. I good fisherman. All my *kane* friends say so. I am *kahuna* of da fish. They jump out of da sea for me." When he laughed, his chunky brown belly bounced.

He was well over three hundred pounds. His cut-off khakis were bursting at the seams. He wore sandals, two bracelets, and a necklace all made of shells. Lawai'a made them himself. He was also proud of his many tattoos. Flexing his mammoth biceps was something else he

143

was proud of. He flexed for Bliss to show his fancy for her. He was boastful, yet shy.

The other women, like Bliss, were chained to the wall. Their lengths of chain were just enough to lie down on the small army surplus cots. They were the midwives.

The young girls were starting to give birth to the first batch. A boat was to arrive soon to take the first of the babies. The next batch would be birthing in less than a month.

He turned his head. Bliss took advantage and gave a heads-up to the others as they watched the two interact. Lawai'a scratched at the loose soil with his sandals. "I can make it good for you, ya?"

"Oh Lawai'a, I make you plenty happy. I make your little *tiki* stand erect like a proud *kahuna*. You like that?"

His face reddened as he grabbed her wrist with the metal cuff and chain. Reaching into his tight khaki front pocket, he produced a small shiny key and released the chain from the wall. Holding on with his huge fat hands, he pulled her out of the chamber along a dimly lit narrow path, yanking on her wrist chain.

As he walked in front, she did her best to keep up. She stumbled along barefoot and used her free hand to brace herself to keep up with him. It was the same path they took days earlier. Without a watch, calendar, or even a glimpse of sunlight, time was hard to gauge. For Bliss and the others, the endless days and nights had melded into one long, continuous nightmare. The constant threats and malnourishment left her and the others too weak to function. It sapped their strength, their life.

Padding along the dark narrow pathway, they soon reached a wider area of the tube. It was a dimly lit abandoned chamber once used for communications. An aluminum three-inch conduit containing the electric, coax, and telephone cables ran along the floor.

Several small cubicles lined the side walls. A few stations had computers and other data equipment, though most had been dismantled and moved. Tremors and ceiling cave-ins had made that room too dangerous to work in.

The communications were set up farther down the line. The roof was crumbling; fallen chunks of jagged lava rock lay helter-skelter.

As before, Lawai'a stopped to talk with the two guards posted at both ends of the chamber. Like him, they were big Island men. Unlike him, they were not Samoan.

Again he clamped her metal wrist cuff to one of the dusty tables in an unlit cubicle. The three guards headed out the other end of the chamber. Luna, the biggest one, held up a doobie, laughing.

At the cubicle next to Bliss was a crumpled-looking PC that had been hit by falling rock. She stretched and contorted her body around and with the big toes of both feet she nudged it to the edge of the table. She righted herself and leaned, just barely reaching it with her free hand. She was strong enough to lift it set it down in front of her. An electrical cord was not far away.

CHAPTER TWENTY-FIVE

Over The Pacific

"Okay Gordy. Let's go back to the seminary. This caper has a link to it. Look at the facts. A, you and Kat come back here for a seminar. B, your hotel just happens to be up the road from good ole Capital City Seminary.

"We *won* that battle. We never rested. Why?"

Gordon rustled in his seat. Mick was making him think. He knew his partner was about to align the ducks, so he played along. "I dunno. Why, Mick?"

"We let one fish get away," Mick answered.

Gordon answered. "How could we have known?"

"And our own special family. Pam Darling. She got to the heart of the matter, and how! Nurse Anne, the brainy one. That leaves Lloyd. He was good."

Gordon fell into his trap. "Lloyd and I had more in common than we realized. We had a system, too."

"Saved a lot of kids in our day," Mick said. "We lost a couple along the way. That eats at my guts, too. But we did what police agencies couldn't do. We got the scummy bastards. Then there's your buddy, William."

"I'm a little tired, if you don't mind, Mick," Gordon answered stiffly.

"You haven't heard from William on this caper, have you?" Mickey asked, but Gordon was already half-asleep.

Mickey shook it off and reminisced to himself as Gordon nodded off in the deep leather chair next to him. He had gone undercover in the past to gain access to groups of pedophiles–scout leaders, teachers, kiddy-porn dealers, bad CPS agencies, caseworkers and other douche-bags that preyed on kids.

Gordon played it straight, out in the open. Together, they were a team to be reckoned with. Outgunned, out-numbered, outsmarted most of the time, and yet they always got the job done.

Mick's thoughts turned to M.G. He stood and tapped her on the shoulder motioning her to follow. They stepped toward the galley in the middle of the first class section. "How'd you get set up as Betz's nurse? Straight up, now."

She answered readily. "An out-of-work male nurse in his late twen-ties spotted an ad in the paper for a physician's assistant in an office setting. That was about four months ago. He applied for the job and got it.

"His body was discovered in a courtyard in the Kiva Center on Fifth Avenue, in Old Town Scottsdale. He was found facedown in a water fountain surrounded by palm trees. The cops did a little checking on it and ruled the death suspicious.

"Happens a lot in the Phoenix Valley," she went on with a shrug. "The police out there are grossly understaffed. If you're looking to kill somebody, that's the place to do it. Felons go there to hide, witness protection people–folks like that.

"Anyway, agents scanned the police report and looked into the doctor's credentials. Guess what? All of his records turned out to be bogus, including his name.

"Everything hit a dead end. And those dead ends led to his being washed out of the CIA and the FBI. And his name, though, that was the tricky thing. Where the name Aaron Betz ended, another cropped up. One name came up in his past, Paul Cheney. That's when they contacted me."

The hair on Mickey's neck stood on end. "Paul Cheney was a Catholic bishop in Capital City. Gordy and I chased him down."

"A pedophile, right?" she asked.

Mick nodded.

"Okay," she said. "So, you know that my friends and I hunt those kinds of rump-rangers. That's when the FBI contacted me. He put in another ad. I answered it and became his assistant. He's very aloof, egotistical, bigoted, and very much a woman hater.

"I got that much from him the first nine minutes on the job. Those traits aren't illegal. Too bad ignorance isn't punishable. All we had on him was that he was a quack. I wanted more. After the name Paul Cheney came another name, Father Lawrence Burke. That name ring a bell?"

Mickey squinted, rubbing his forehead with his thumb and middle finger. "Yeah, it does. A shadowy figure, knows when to stay and when to leave. Never shows his face. Been wanting to get him for too long."

"Glad you brought that up." Mickey shot her a look. She explained. "Yeah, His face – hardly any whiskers, feminine in a way. He's a tall, thin guy, tattooed thin black eyebrows, not much hair on him and I swear he's had more face-lifts than Michael Jackson."

Mick's brows bounced. "Where is he?"

"If I knew ..." She paused mid-sentence and thought a bit. "We're on the right trail. I may have a connection in Hawaii, an old crazy Viet Nam vet. Worth a shot. I'll check with my group. How old is that slippery fuck, anyway?"

"Damn good question," Mick said. "Nobody seems to know."

M.G. finished, saying, "Anyway, that's when I got in contact with our mutual friend, Richard Fleming. He's the one who filled me in on Maggie and you guys, just before he passed."

Mickey nodded. Glancing back to their cabin, he saw that Kat had taken his seat next to Gordon, who rested his head on her shoulder. Running her fingers through his hair, Kat looked past her partner of fifty-plus years to the aqua-blue waters thirty-seven thousand feet below. There was a tear in her eye.

CHAPTER TWENTY-SIX

Down The Tubes

L awai'a sat on the black lava rock gazing at the soft waves out to the anchored three-tiered cruise ship. Alongside him were his two *kane koas* inhaling a Maui Wowie. Grown on Maui, it was smooth, not harsh on the lungs as mainland marijuana often is. This went down easy; it made his mind go *hau'oli*. With each giggle, his tanned rubbery blubber rolled.

The one called Lio, the Hawaiian name for horse, stood and teetered, then charged hard toward the sea. His long black hair danced behind him as he galloped to the edge of the lava and dove into the warm aqua-blue waters. He was the tallest and fittest of the trio.

Luna, the one who called himself the boss, sat next to Lawai'a. They watched Lio as he swam along the jagged shoreline. Luna held higher rank within the little *hui* of guards. They were known as *koas* to the elders, the *'elemakule kahuna*. The *haole* in charge was a white American. He did business here from the mainland.

The soldiers didn't like him or his woman friend. They respected him out of fear, however, and he paid them wages not seen on the Islands. They obeyed. The money was too good to pass up. Now there was another *haole* standing in for the short, brown-haired boss. The new white man was crazy with power.

If anyone were caught taking free time as they were, they would be punished severely. The *koas,* the soldiers, knew this, but they also knew Hawaiian ways. There's always tomorrow. They took their time, Hawaiian time. It was in their blood. No *haole* was going to take that away.

Luna glanced at Lawai'a, smiling, sitting next to him. "You like the doobie? Has ecstasy added for good measure. Maybe your *tiki* be happy now."

Lawai'a blushed and stood up. "Ya, he happy. Little *tiki* getting bigger." Lawai'a laughed. Lio caught the gist of the conversation as he came back from his cool swim. He grinned as he caught his breath.

Luna didn't laugh. He took a short toke for show. He was in the business of selling it, not smoking it. It was a side job, at least until he had his fill of the elderly *haole* from the mainland.

Luna was one of the first recruits. He liked the feeling that power brings. He was going to rule the drug business in Hawaii someday; he had no doubts about that.

He used the money to buy acres of land. The land was fertile and the business was good. It wasn't going to be long before he said aloha to the rest of the *kaos,* and leave the Big Island for Maui.

Besides, he didn't like the fact that they were using the throw-away girls from the seedy sections of Honolulu for the baby factory. He was born in one of those hoods, amid the garbage and stench.

He was a survivor and strong because of it. He made his way out because he was smart and could think fast on his feet–faster than the others. His friends had all died young.

"Time to get back to work," Luna said. Lawai'a and Lio followed him up the narrow, winding path to the small opening behind the jagged bush. They stooped and entered the lava tube. Lio saw the path he took several days earlier. "Hey, ever been down there?" he asked, pointing to a dark footpath off to one side.

Luna stiffened. "No one is to enter that sacred place. It is *kapu!* You must be with a true *kahuna* only." He hoped he'd made himself clear.

He'd heard from others that it was a death cave, a place of ancient burial grounds. Luna had not seen it himself and didn't want to. He didn't like the sight of bones anyway. If he had a weakness, Luna was afraid of spirits and tales of the afterlife.

Loi slouched a tad. He didn't want to show his displeasure. He respected Luna, but not his superstitious nature. Why, Luna even flinched at the mention of the *Menehune,* the little ones of lore. Some called them elves, yet others said they were the original children of Hawaii, and of the world. To Lio, it was just the Hawaiian version of the Garden of Eden. He didn't care what Luna thought about graves, the *Menehune,* or anything else.

Loi wanted to experience the death caves, see what it felt like just being there. That's all. To set foot in the sacred chambers of ancient Hawaiians and see them in their battle gear–that was his goal. Lio had heard stories. He had walked that way before. As one got to the end of the path, there was a ledge. He could see it but not reach it. He could jump and touch the ledge but he couldn't hang on.

What was on the other side? That was what he wanted to know and see–to experience the gods of his ancestors! Only a few had set foot in a death cave, and Lio wanted to be counted among those few.

Beads of moisture dripped from the ceiling cones here and there as they got farther in. The ground shook suddenly. They stopped. "Madam Pele doing the hula?" Lawai'a asked out loud.

"Oh, ya. She make hula when she's angry," Lio answered. "Some days two, maybe three times." He pointed up at a small fissure where hot steam whistled through. They glanced at one another. The smell of sulphur filled the air.

Luna quickened his pace. The whiff of it smelled like rotten eggs. They galloped through the winding tube towards the chamber where he had left Bliss.

She heard them coming. The tremor startled her. A crack grew along the wall near the top of the chamber and small chunks of rock fell to the tables and floor. She didn't have time to unplug the computer before her captors arrived. Instead she flipped the electrical cord to the floor, out of sight. The three entered the room running.

They stopped at the entrance and looked around. Swirls of yellowish-orange dust from the light of the oil lamps gave the place an eerie glow. Steam rolled and hissed from the cracks in the wall.

Lawai'a stepped toward Bliss and unlocked her from the table. He moved quick and ungraceful as he reached for her. At the same time the computer fell to the floor. A red light flashed, catching Luna's eyes.

He peered at Lawai'a. "Fool! You left her at a computer table. What were you thinking?" He moved in, and picked up the laptop and set it back on the table. The blinking stopped before he set it down.

"Were you on the computer, woman?" Luna shouted.

She stared down at the floor. She had learned to do that in her five months of captivity. To look her captors in the eye was a sign of defiance, a sign of presumed equality; it wasn't a good idea to show them strength. To lower ones eyes was a form of submission, to let them know that they held the power.

"Answer me, bitch!" he continued.

To lie now and be caught would mean severe punishment. The PC could have blinked because of the fall, she reasoned, yet it was the same light that blinks when it closes down. It hadn't completely shut down when they arrived.

They had returned so suddenly and she hadn't expected that; Luna knew that as well. She had seen him use a computer in that very chamber. What was more, she knew he had used it without anyone else knowing about it. He was making contact with someone on the outside.

"Yes. I tried," she admitted. "Unlike you, I don't know the password to get in. I tried to shut it off before you came back. Lawai'a didn't notice the computer on the other desk." She made a head movement toward Lawai'a. He nodded in agreement.

"That's right. She had to. There was no computer at that desk, Luna."

Luna saw the defiance in Lawai'a's eyes. "So, you *are* protecting her? For what?"

"Big fisherman, you plan on giving the *haole wahine* the big boom-boom when you get the chance, ya? You dog, you! Too much ecstasy in that doobie for you to handle? Maybe you should drop your pants and make boom-boom now while Lio and I watch."

The fisherman's eyes widened as he saw the fire in Luna's. He was embarrassed. Luna wasn't kidding. He wanted him to have sex with Bliss, right now as they watched. How could he get out of it?

"Now, fisherman! Take off your shorts. Bend her over the table—now!" His voice had changed. It became distinct and deliberate. With a sneer he added, "And when you're finished, Lio and I will try it out."

Lawai'a felt embarrassed for himself and for Bliss. However, he had no choice, so he obeyed. He squirmed out of his tight shorts and kicked them aside. Lio felt sorry for him, but he couldn't pull rank on Luna, not now, especially in front of a woman. He sat on a table and said nothing.

The fisherman pulled the t-shirt off of Bliss, and clutched the sides of her cream-colored pajama bottoms and yanked them down. Turning her around, he leaned her face down on the table. He touched her warm ass with his fingers, then his hands slid around her buns as if he were massaging them.

He stood close to her, feeling his *tiki* against her warm skin. His heart raced. He was excited. His *tiki* grew and hardened. He pushed it under her cheeks and thrust forward. She tightened, not letting him in. He pushed harder and harder. With his knees he forcefully bumped her legs apart. He was ready to ejaculate. Crazy with anticipation, he grabbed her hard and went at her again.

Poor Lawai'a was so excited that he climaxed without gaining entry. He faked the rest, backing away a bit, pumping his arm high as if he were successful finishing the job.

Bliss closed her legs together as the white creamy fluid dripped off her to the floor. She looked back to the others. She could see Luna preparing himself to be next.

"God, send me an angel of protection," she breathed softly. She shed no tears. Resigned to her fate, she readied herself for what was to come. She too was a survivor. She was a Marine. It was in her genes.

Luna stepped toward her and pulled her up facing him. "You ain't been *had* until you been had by me, *bitch.*" He slapped the defenseless Bliss hard across the face with both hands once, then again and again.

Grabbing her hair with a tight fist, he yanked her back on the desk, slamming her head down on it fast and hard. Dizziness overtook her. She began seeing things in slow motion. Her head ached. She saw stars.

Luna spit on one hand, rubbing it on the end of his *tiki* as he stepped toward her. He leaned and raised her bare legs up and over his shoulders. Pressing up against her, he began to enter her.

She screamed. A sudden tremor jolted the chamber. Large chunks of the ceiling gave way. A huge jagged boulder fell, slamming the back of Luna's head. It crushed his skull. White matter and blood both sprayed and oozed. Bliss reeled in horror as she pushed his body off of her.

"Fuck, brah. What we gonna do?" The fisherman panicked. Before Lio could answer, there was another tremor. Lio could only think of one thing–surviving.

With a jerk of his head he shouted, "Grab her! Take her back to her quarters. I'll make up a story. I must tell Lilia, the *wahine* in charge of the soldiers. I must tell her about Luna. Hurry!"

Lio sped along the tube, heading for Lilia's chamber. Lawai'a struggled in his tight cut-offs as he pushed the naked, dazed woman toward the room for the midwives. Bliss was covered with Luna's blood and small clumps of brain matter.

She moved like an automaton, feeling nothing. Nothing seemed real in this underground world. The blood and gray matter that plastered her hair, arms, and upper body made her feel trapped in a living nightmare. The left side of her face felt strangely hot.

She touched it with the back of her free hand. Blood. She traced the hot spot with a finger. There was a long, narrow gash in her face from her cheekbone down to the corner of her upper lip. Red crimson dripped from her face to her shoulder.

Another tremor rolled–harder this time as more chunks from the rocky ceiling gave way, crashing down on everything, including the crushed body of Luna. The legs of the desk bent and crumpled. Piles of rocks all but closed both entrances. The old communications chamber began to take the appearance of a ancient, forgotten tomb.

They scrambled along the narrow pathway as the ceiling dribbled warm droplets of water and the floor gushed with steam. The air was heavy with the stink of sulphur.

Lio was bleeding too. His leg was gashed from falling rock. He pulled a white kerchief from his back pocket, ripped it, and tied it around the open wound as he limped through the lava tube. He had to report to the woman he feared.

***

In a far chamber deep inside the underground passageways, Aaron sat with Lilia at a small round wooden table.

"These tremors have been getting stronger," she said. As the room shook, their eyes met and she paused, saying nothing for a moment, then: "They're happening with regularity. It's a bad sign. Legend has it that when the ground rumbles, Madam Pele is angry about something so she shakes her hips. When the people please her, she stops. She's not happy now."

Stone-faced, Aaron said, "Perhaps she's on the rag. It stinks. The odor is sickening. She's been spewing the hot molten rock here for what, twenty years, now?

"This is the newest part of the Islands," he went on. "It happens. Don't get me wrong–I am concerned. We've just started our little operation, Lilia. We've a long way to go. We cannot stay here forever. Always on the move is the way to forever, don't forget that.

"I've been at it a long time," he continued with a weary sigh, "and I don't plan on altering the course now. Opus Dei. God's work. We're on the right path. I sense a crack within our loyal guards. We'll have to move our base of operations soon."

Lilia reached across the table, putting her hand on top of his cold bony one. She felt the quiver and removed her hand from his.

The man was getting old. Physically, he seemed to be in good shape. He kept himself fit. He ate raw fruits, fresh fish, and vegetables. No dairy products or junk food in his strict regimen.

She knew more than she let on, though. She recognized his symptoms even if he didn't. Parkinson's. It was getting worse. Soon, she thought sadly, she'll have to eliminate him. *Business*, she thought.

Aaron sat staring straight ahead. He folded his hands, looking down at them, not moving his head. He thought for a moment, *Who would carry on if not for me?* Opening his hands, shifting his eyes to see Lilia now standing next to him.

She put a gentle hand on his shoulder as if to say, "I understand." Instead, she said, "You're needed here, Aaron. The FLOC couldn't survive without you. The LOC will always remain true. The fundamental concept has been with us for thousands of years.

"It's by God's design that it survives for another thousand years," she continued. "History has shown us that the Church cannot do it alone. It needs its foot soldiers, Aaron, and like you, it needs unwavering leadership. Uniting with others gets easier every day, thanks to the Internet."

With a frail voice he said, "I miss the gatherings, Lilia. There was a time we could meet openly. In many counties, we still can."

He smiled a bittersweet smile, a smile conveying the ache for a bygone time. "The kiddie sex tours in Thailand and Singapore are very accommodating," he went on. "Brazil, as well, but they're so far away. Yes, there are still the house-to-house gatherings. I miss the big meetings though, the weeklong affairs with the others, out in the open, not ashamed. Can we still be who we are?"

Lilia stepped behind him and massaged his neck and shoulders. She slid her hands down inside his shirt to his chest. With the practiced movement of a professional massage therapist she rubbed her hands along his ribcage, pulling up on his chest with his nipples between her fingers. His breasts felt warm and inviting.

She leaned closer, kissing his cheek and ear. He tilted his head toward hers. "I'm going to my room and get the updates from our soldiers," she said softly.

He turned and watched the only woman he had ever let into his life drift through the narrow archway. She was much younger than he. He liked the little-girl look she still had in her eyes and her pouting lips. She reminded him of his first sexual encounter, the one with the eight-year-old girl. He was barely twenty at the time.

Lilia was petite, yet physically able to bring down a big man with her karate chops and leg kicks. He had seen her in action. She snapped the neck of a policeman in the Chinatown section of Honolulu not long ago. How proud he had been! And in so doing, she saved him from being jailed.

She was stern and sensual with the children, too. Aaron watched her take on two teenaged boys one night. She donned her leathers and initiated the lads in the art of S&M, *all* night long. He loved it. But by God, he thought, she *lives* for it!

The broken phone rang.

CHAPTER TWENTY-SEVEN

Honolulu International Airport

"**...** *ust landed. I'll wait for the others. They were detained in Dallas. I'll keep you informed.*"

"Yes, you do that," Aaron said, and hung up the phone. His hands, once steady and smooth, began to twitch. The tremors were more persistent now, both in his hands and in the caves.

Nothing was going to stop him now. He was no quitter, damn it! Deep inside he was still Larry, the tall boy who looked older than his age. As a teenager, he looked to Paul Cheney as his mentor.

Now at his computer, he banged away at the keys:

I wish Father Paul were here to see how I, like Peter, have become a rock among men. I am the standard by which others are judged.

Through the Internet we strengthen the ties that bind us all. We must, however, become more vocal. The re-education of children should not be a sin, nor should it be a crime. We need lobbyists to reach key politicians; we need to get our hands in the pockets of more congressmen and senators. Our government is at its weakest now.

We must demand weaker pornography laws now! Perhaps now we can succeed. With a born-againer as president, the right wing is in its religious glory, oh halleluiah! The rest of the country is oblivious. Religious fervor is at its apex.

Now is the time to unite and expand the FLOC. The cause is just, and mucho money to be had. The children belong to us. God bless the self-righteous religious!

Aaron thought of a time when he was young, and stopped typing. He'd climbed a tree in front of his house one hot summer night. From there he watched his parents make love while his six-month-old baby sister lay naked in the same bed.

Was that the defining moment then that his sexual fantasies included children? He had tried to shake the memory from his mind, but the more he tried, the stronger the urge to relive it became. Eventually he saw only children in his fantasies. Soon, he couldn't distinguish fantasy from reality.

Then his father introduced him to an acquaintance of his, a priest from Wisconsin. Father Paul Cheney was invited to stay a week at his home. Larry's father insisted. It was there that young Larry was indoctrinated in the ways of the Legionnaires of the Christo.

He never returned to his father's house, or back to Wisconsin for that matter, unless a child was involved. Lawrence Burke took more than their innocence; he also took their lives. He snuffed them all save for one, an eight-year-old.

Over the years he and his rich and powerful friends persuaded key political figures to stay clear of the adoption agencies. The less information on the biological parents, the easier it was for his group to satisfy their desires and twist the minds of innocent children.

He found Arizona and its weak laws an ideal environment for his psycho-sexual predilections to thrive. He became a regional manager for the Child Protective Services in Tucson. Moving the kids from one agency to another, then to foster homes and foster care facilities, and finally from house to house, swapping kids, one for another. It was a beautiful and elegant scheme that worked so well for the LOC.

Over time the system fails. It loses track of the kids and to cover it up, their names are removed from ledgers and nobody's the wiser. It's a simple game, really, still used with impunity today in states where there's a minimum of tax dollars allocated for the care and protection of children.

Giggling to himself, Aaron resumed typing:

Where did the kids come from, and where did they go? To the streets, my pretty, to the streets, to live, to rot, to die. Throw-away—throw-away, throw-a-way, all!

CHAPTER TWENTY-EIGHT

2:30 PM - Somewhere Over the Pacific

T he flight became bumpy. The passengers bounced like popcorn in a hot popper, some spilling out of their seats. The flight attendants teetered, tipping their food trays; Mai Tai's sailed through the air as earphones were tuned to Don Ho singing "Tiny Bubbles."

"Jesus H. Christ!" a drunk shouted in the coach section, *"Who* th' fuck's driving this goddam thing, anyway?"

Gordon tightened his belt, as did the others. "M.G.," he said, leaning over in his buckled seat, "in the chapel this morning you were chanting. Around the altar where the woman lay, you were doing something else, what was that?"

M.G. lowered her copy of *The Funny Times,* a satirical monthly. Clutching the arms of the seat she answered his question simply: "Channeling."

"Really?" Gordon bit at his upper lip for a second as he thought. "You think you could hone in on our friend, Aaron Betz?"

"Already have," she said, and the words spilled out fast and furious. "Like a cat with nine lives, ol' Aaron moves on, doesn't stay in one place too long. He works at night, sleeps little, stays out of sight. A loner, and prefers it that way. Has ties to no one, yet loyal to a fault. Victimized as a child. Love-hate relationship with children, men, and there's something odd and obscene in his relationships with women. He's afraid of 'em—their power and influence."

Gordon nodded. Mickey too was utterly absorbed in every word as she continued:

"He wants what women have, but he doesn't know how to get it. He loves the power of pedophilia. He has a deadly fascination with children; likes to watch others in sexual play, too.

"Would like nothing better than a young boy, say five, six or seven, yet strangely he has S&M fantasies with women who take charge.

"That oddly contradicts with his belief system because *he* must be in charge, *always*. Like, he could be a priest and hear confessions, yet have the urge to slit someone's throat. He likes knives, sharp knives. And taunting, he *loves* taunting."

"Jesus," Mickey muttered under his breath.

"He's articulate. Intelligent. But aloof, with grandiose plans for a 'great society.' Like Stalin, Hitler, David Koresh, Reverend Jim Jones–sweeties like that. He feels he's been ordained as the Chosen One, to carry on with his grand schemes.

"One other thing, guys. I see him tremble. I don't know what that means. Perhaps it's symbolic, like he's on shaky ground in a figurative sense, or he's in danger or–maybe he's ill. He thinks he may die or have to move quickly. I don't understand that part. Only he can tell us. I'm at a loss for words on that."

***

"Unless there's a new eruption somewhere else," Mick said, "I'd say the volcano we're looking for is Kilauea, maybe inside Volcano National Park itself."

Gordon uncrossed his legs, took his hand off his chin, and said, "Well deduced, Doctor Watson. I suppose the entrance to the lava tube we're looking for is inside the ranger station. Or maybe it's under the men's shitter, waiting for us to waltz in and nab the whole bunch, whoever the hell they are.

"Let's say we get lucky and he *is* on the Big Island," Gordon went on. "That would put the operation on the Hilo side." He waited for someone to chime in, but no one did. He looked to the others. "Any ideas? Thoughts?"

They'd hit a dead end. Mick said, "Hopefully we'll know more once we land. We can contact the FBI, and M.G. can check with her family for leads."

Gordon wisecracked, "You could buy a Hawaiian shirt when we get there. You won't have to tuck it in."

Mickey flipped him the bird. "Or you could shove this up your ass and spin around on it for a while."

"Boys, boys, boys," M.G. sighed, then looked to Kat. "How do you put up with these clowns?"

"Easy. I act like I don't know them." She shook her head as she stared down Gordon. "Or I just grab his credit cards and go on a retail therapy binge." M.G. laughed. Gordon didn't.

"I'm going back to the seminary, to Larry," Gordon said.

"Yeah," Mickey replied through a sigh. "First time we met, he and I, you cold-cocked him." Mickey winced, shaking his head at the memory. "We had him, too. The bastard just slipped away. No one ever explained that one—how he got out and vanished like that—poof!"

Gordon nodded in agreement. "Chameleons change colors to blend in, survive. What changes did he make?"

***

Far back in a connecting cave, Aaron stood in front of a mirror attached to the rocky wall. He examined his tattooed eyebrows on his near-hairless, re-sculptured face.

Oil lamps along the walls gave flickering light to the cool but dank ten-by-twelve-foot room. Water dripped from the stalactites. He had a tarp placed over the wettest spot. Ultimately all the waters drifted downward from the lava tubes toward the deep blue sea.

Aaron sat back down at the computer and typed:

And they're coming to take me away, ha-ha, they're coming to take me away ho-ho, he-hee, to the funny farm. The nice men in their long white coats are coming to take me away, aha, ho-ho, hehee ...

Aaron half smiled as the lyrics from a long-lost novelty record played through his head. He was thinking of his pursuers. Gordon and Mickey had been on his ass for fifty years.

Then another lyric, this time from a Chuck Berry classic whistled through his mind: *"No you can't catch me, 'cause if you get too close, I'll be gone like a cool breeze."*

He banged away on the keyboard, glancing up from time to time at the screen in front of him. Aaron was getting old, but he kept his body young. He practiced yoga. He ate right and stayed in shape. His body was strong.

He hammered on, *They might catch me and they might not. Kurt is on the job. I taught the fool what I could....*

His thoughts eventually took him away from typing. Sometime not too long into the future, he mused, I must write down my exploits while working in the Child Protective Services in Tucson. Easiest cash I ever made and lots of it! The trips with my special cargo to Taos, New Mexico; the kiddie market was so profitable there with the clergy and their special friends from Rome.

The real money was made over the past fifteen years through charities. Because of my plan, the beloved LOC took in hundreds of millions both here and abroad. All of it from the sale of children.

And all through the miracle of the Internet. He laughed at the thought. It was more of a cackle, like a hen laying an oversized egg. FMCC. Feed My Christian Children, ACCR-American Child Cancer Research, DCOV-Disabled Children Of Veterans, and several other charities, all under one umbrella, the LOC. *I lead the way,* he reflected, and another cackle from deep in his throat echoed through the rocky corridors. He hammered on the keyboard again.

However, it shall have to wait. It is time for contingency plans. This place of sanctuary is crumbling. We must move soon, I fear. This nonsense about the goddess of volcanoes, Madam Pele, is for tribal people, simple-minded oafs. A female god? How primitive. But this is a primitive place, to be sure.

The Hawaiian folklore teems with idiotic superstitions. Is it any wonder the Church of the Latter-day Saints is converting these foolish Polynesians, island by island?

My beloved Catholic Church missed the boat here. But, so many souls to save in the south central Americas, I can understand; more people, more oil, means more money. Even the evangelicals are gaining their share of the market down there. Oil, black gold, Texas tea ...

And then there's Gordon. I knew where he came from.

CHAPTER TWENTY-NINE

Ten Minutes Later

G ordon sat on the too-small commode to catch his breath. He'd taken another trip to the john at the back of the plane to stretch his aching legs. Getting up, he ran the hot water faucet and stared at the dried water spots on the mirror. *William, where the hell are you?*

He was thinking of his buddy, the little one who grew up to be a strapping fifteen-year-old. "I found out where you came from, you know," he said aloud to the mirror. "Lloyd told me. He had to pay to find out, but he told me that *and* something else. Guess where *he* came from? And me? You've been too quiet. What the hell are you doing?"

Either his breath or the hot water fogged up the mirror in the tiny space-perhaps both. Whatever the case, words now appeared scribbled on the mirror. "That can't be!" He squeezed his disbelieving eyes shut and reopened them. On the cloudy surface of the mirror were these words:

Maggot: A soft-bodied legless larva, esp. that of a fly found in decaying matter.

Swiping at the hand towel dispenser, he wiped the mirror clean. When he did the cloud-like mist over took the tiny space in the lavatory again, *except* for the mirror.

Gordon wiped at the mirror again, as if that would clear the room of the fog. Instead a face began to appear in the mirror. It was the face of his young friend, William. And he spoke:

"Hi, boss. Long time, no see."

Gordon's jaw dropped and beads of sweat formed on his forehead. He sat down on the commode, shaking his head.

"Gordy, you ole snake-in-the-grass, it's good to see you again!"

Gordon wiped the sweat off of his forehead with a tissue and said, "Will, we could sure use your help here. We need to get correct information on the exact whereabouts of Margaret's daughter, Bliss, and we need it ASAP. This is big, my friend. Maybe it's too big, for us–for me."

"I'll be blunt, Gordy. We've been listening in on the conversations for the past twenty-four hours."

Gordon didn't look into the mirror as Will spoke. Not because he was afraid, but because of the pains in his chest. Staring down at the floor, he said, "I'm in trouble, Will. My ticker, it's, it's–"-

Will didn't give him a chance to finish. Instead he interrupted by saying, *"She's about to call for help. You have to do as I say. Got it?"*

Gordon nodded, not looking up.

William continued, *"When the plane lands, I want you to send Kathryn back to Capital City. Chloe needs her. Things have changed. Anyway, the Big Island is too dangerous for her.*

"Listen to Mick, as well as M.G., and for God's sake, follow your instincts. M.G. can provide the weapons and yes, I know how you feel about guns, but just do it. Trust your gut. I'll see you soon."

Gordon remained on the commode as he tried to take it all in, then suddenly his mind went blank. He was about to say something, but he paused before he asked one final question. "What do you mean, I'll see you soon?"

William pushed his face forward through the mirror and opened his mouth. Maggots fell into the sink.

The fog instantly cleared. Gordon took another tissue.

A minute later, Mickey turned and looked up as Gordon made his way back to his seat, clutching something in his hand. He handed the folded tissue to Mickey, who opened it carefully with his forefinger and thumb. Examining the maggots, he asked, "Who?"

Gordon shook his head. "William."

CHAPTER THIRTY

3:35 Hawaii Time, August 13th

"Where did this happen, Lio?" she asked. The young soldier traipsed through the tubes with Lilia close behind. Passing through the birthing room and washing area, they stopped. A narrow waterfall above the oval-shaped chamber spouted fresh water into a rounded-out basin. Lawai'a was washing Bliss with a sponge.

"What's going on here?" Lilia demanded. The fisherman feared the *haole wahine*. Stammering, he glanced to Lio, then to Lilia, and back to Lio, who explained, "I ordered him to wash her and to take her back with the others."

Lilia looked into the gaunt gray skin and hollow eyes of the naked woman. With angry eyes and a grip of steel, she grabbed Bliss by the arm, shouting, "Did you kill my soldier—my number-one soldier? Talk, you bitch, before I have this man drown you in this bloody cave. You hear me, cunt? *Speak up!*"

With as much strength as she could muster, Bliss spat out, "Ooh-rah," before her knees buckled. She tried not to fall, but her legs betrayed her.

"Pick her up, you ignorant brown-skin," screamed Lilia "Now!"

Lawai'a did as he was told. Bliss seemed disconnected and barely coherent.

Lilia asked her again, "How did this happen?"

Bliss opened her mouth and in a throaty murmur said, "He raped me. The sky fell. He died on top of me." She turned her face to show Lilia the gash on her face.

Lilia turned to Lawai'a. He nodded. She then pierced Lio's eyes with her angry glare. "Well? Is it true?"

He stood more erect as he searched for the right words. "That's correct Ms. Lilia, Luna wanted Lawai'a to enter her first, to watch, and then he wanted her for himself.

"That's when the shaking happened." Lio broke in. "Did you not feel it where you were?"

Of course she had felt it. She was sitting across from Aaron at the time. It was an omen–a bad omen, and she knew it.

"He should not have done that." Lilia said. "Not to this woman. He went too far. And now Madam Pele is ready to spew her anger."

She turned to Lio and said, "You did the right thing by coming to me. You are the *kanaka ikaika.* As the most important soldier, you'll be in charge of the others now. You must protect the *hapai* women, those who are pregnant. Did I say that right?"

Both soldiers nodded in agreement. Lilia went on, "You shall have the honor of guarding them with your life, if necessary. Am I clear on that?"

Once again they nodded. Showing Lio that she meant business, she called Lawai'a a fool in Hawaiian. *"Hupo,* dry her off and take her to the *haole kahuna* now. I want Lio with me, alone."

Lilia stepped toward Lio. He knew he was about to be tested. Just how ... he didn't know.

As Lawai'a pushed Bliss out of the shower room, Lilia ordered Lio to follow her up the narrow winding pathway. Suddenly she stopped, reached out and put her warm hand firmly on his bare chest.

"I know you think things were better here before the haole white man came back to take charge," she said in a low voice, adding, "Get over it."

She pushed him again. He felt the sharp edge of a rock at his thick calves as she applied pressure to his broad shoulders. He sat down on the rough stone ledge on the side of the basin. Lilia was dressed only in her orange flowered black muumuu that draped to her ankles.

She hoisted it up to her waist as she leaned forward and pulled his face to her thighs. "Just follow my instructions. I'll let you know when I've had enough."

***

Lawai'a sat Bliss down on her cot and covered her nakedness with the bed sheet. He was gentle and sat next to her. "I'm sorry for what happened, and angry, too. I do not like to be made a fool of. That *haole* woman means nothing to me, but I must obey. Do you understand? If there were a way, I would release you.

"I am only a fisherman, but you are kind. You do not make a fool of me. You are good woman. I want you to get plenty rest now. I wish to get you good pork to eat, fresh vegetables, too. You'll see. Lawai'a has honor. I'm no child." He leaned in and kissed her cheek and laid her down on the cot. Her tired eyes were already closed.

The others, the midwives, cold and hungry, could only watch as she was carried back to their chamber. Bliss turned their way and pushed her tongue out, dropping the key from her mouth into her hand.

Later, when she awoke, the fisherman fed her fresh pork, fish, and bread.

***

"Lio," Lilia said, "bring that woman here. She has rested and eaten. The big *haole kahuna* wants to see her now. Make sure she is presentable."

As Lio started to leave, she stopped him.

"Just a moment. Don't say a word to Lawai'a. He shows signs of weakness. As for you, Lio, I'm thinking of you as the new *supreme* leader."

Lio stood guard at the entrance to the room. He followed the instructions while making long, proud strides through the pathway that led to the chamber of the midwives.

"Lio," Aaron called to him as he padded along the tube, "make sure you keep Lilia entertained *after* you leave the girl with me."

175

CHAPTER THIRTY-ONE

5:09 PM, August 13th

Aaron ranted. His eyes were blood-red. "I knew your mother when she was eight. Her brother–your uncle Tim–I held him in my arms. Your mother was a strong defender. She intervened on his behalf. She wanted to–save him, shall we say. Ha! She was a mere sacrificial lamb.

"I touched her once, then again, and again." A tight smile knitted its way across his face as he watched the subtle changes in her expression.

He had Bliss chained to the wall of his primitive quarters. Blood had caked around the gash on the side of her face. Her arms were clamped at the wrists above her head, making it difficult to breathe. Her lungs were compressed and she felt as if she was slowly suffocating. She wondered if Jesus had felt something like this, struggling just to breathe, before he died on the cross.

Growing weak, she could do no more and lowered her head. Her arms were outstretched against the rough wall, and her legs were clamped together at the ankles a few inches from the floor. The flames of the crude oil lamps flickered off the ceiling and walls of the cave, casting eerie shadows.

Bliss was close to passing out. Strange, but she thought she could sense a color change in the cold room deep in the cave. Silently, she asked for assistance from the angels. She held out hope, just as she was taught as a young marine. *Never give up,* she told herself, over and over again. *Never give up.*

"I've been studying you," Aaron said to her in a strangely bright, sing-song voice. "Earlier I had wanted to reunite you with a couple of old acquaintances, friends of your mother. Though I doubt you'd remember them."

Looking down to her feet in irons a few inches off the floor, he continued: "I'm not sure how that'll be possible, now. Alas, time is a-wasting.

"You might be comforted to know that as I sit here looking at you nailed to the wall, this rosary I'm praying with was once in the hands of Mother Teresa." He stood and dangled it in front of her face. "Isn't it pretty?"

He waited, but there was no response. Giving a sullen grunt, he paced the room before her.

"I pity you, my child. It's not that I don't want to kill you. I do! Not that it's against my principles, for it is not just that ... but as I look at you there on the wall, hanging and squirming like a stuck pig, I don't think of Jesus. No, I think of razorblades and droplets of blood flying helter-skelter. Making love to a corpse–now, *that's* what excites me.

"You see how it is, don't you?" he said, as he sat on the edge of his chair at the small wooden desk.

He lay the rosary down and reached into his shaving kit next to the small round magnified mirror, and stared at his Gillette Sensor Excel razor, still in its holding tray. Underneath the tray was the built-in plastic container where the five new blades lay in their respective tracts. One was missing, the one presently in the razor.

He touched the sides of the cartridge with his thumb and middle finger and removed it, and set it on the desk next to the mirror.

He ran a thumb and a forefinger across the blade, cutting himself. He put the bloody fingers to his nose and tried to smell his own blood, then placed his digits in his mouth and sucked them clean.

Aaron, AKA Lawrence Burke, stood and walked ever so slowly to Bliss as he began a prayer:

"O my God, I am heartily sorry for having offended Thee, and I detest all my sins because I dread the loss of Heaven and the pains of Hell; but most of all because they offend Thee, my God, Who art all-good and deserving of all my love...."

He continued the Act of Contrition in a peaceful, calm demeanor. He stood before the chained, helpless woman. He raised his hand clutching the razor and made quick, slashing strokes across her body as he continued the prayer:

"I firmly resolve, with the help of Thy grace, to confess my sins, to do penance and to amend my life. Amen."

Blood splattered along the wall and floor next to the chained woman. The warm crimson liquid pooled below her feet.

"Your mother is dead, my pretty thing." He was breathing harder as he continued. "Dead and in a cooler far, far from here. She was the first and I let her live to suffer that special torment of the abused. The others, I took. I had to end it. Don't you see? I teased her all her life, kept her haunted, damaged and fearful. It was time for her to die. Now, it's your turn."

He stopped the slashing and set the razor on the table. He pulled a small jackknife from his front pocket.

Standing in front of Bliss, with his hands and forearms covered in blood, he tried once to pull out the small knife blade. It slipped out of his blood-slicked hands and dropped on the crusty floor. The blade hit first, snapping off the pointed tip. He picked it up and made a quick lunge with the broken edge of the blade toward Bliss' face.

She did the only thing she could do. She jerked her head up and away from the oncoming shiny blade. It didn't help; it pierced her skin below her chin. He drove it all the way in, just missing her throat pipe and artery. Blood spurted, then quickly slowed to a drip before it slowed to clot.

"God, how I love that." Panting, he set the knife down next to the used razor cartridge on his desk. He reached for a pitcher of water from his desk.

He poured water on one hand, and the other, washing the spilt blood, but the blood pooled afresh in his palms and fingers. The red stuff mixed with the water (like the priest mixing water and wine, he reflected), and dripped steadily to the floor.

Rage replaced the calm and gentle demeanor he had a moment ago. He turned to Bliss again with the razor.

Instinctively, the marine in her took over. She stared back at him. Lawrence sensed something different and strange in his trapped prey; he watched it as it struggled for freedom.

Her eyes became cat-like, changing shape and color. Yellow replaced the small black pupils as her eyebrows arched. It was as if *she* had become the stalker.

Lawrence readied himself for the challenge. Now, more than ever, he wanted to decapitate her–slowly. Yet something gnawed at him. Unsure of the uneasy feeling that swelled inside him, he challenged Bliss with it.

He said, "You'll never guess who I have as male nurses tending to the new mothers. You've seen them, I'm sure. My breeders. They're friends of your mother, they are. Old friends of mine, too. Not that it matters. Weak backbones, both of them. Too bad your mother isn't around any more. I'd have liked to see the look on her face when she saw them.

"You don't know who I'm talking about do you?" The ploy didn't work. The demeanor of the woman chained to the wall became even more intense. The woman's rage had taken over any vestige of fear. He hated that.

But, then, Bliss froze. *Who the hell is he talking about?*

"He stepped back from her and said, "They thought of your mother as a cold fish. That's their words, dearie, not mine. Though I suspect she tried her best to please them. Sadly, she failed.

"Your father likes young ones—five, six, seven-year-olds. Can't blame him, really. I've had my share, too."

He eased open a drawer from his wooden desk and pulled out a long narrow object. Blood oozed from his hands, arms, and chest as he opened it. He showed Bliss what a straight razor looked like.

Grinning in a most foul way, he said, "Do you recall seeing one of these?" He put it to the light so she could clearly see the long, thin blade with the metal grip.

"It's used for shaving whiskers off one's face and neck. It's no longer used in today's barbershops. Bacteria, germs, you know ...

"Used in my day, though. Still use it occasionally myself. I taught many a man how to use a straight razor on their, ah, 'clients,' shall we say. I believe, my pretty, that a knife was used on your poor mother, over and over again just a day or so ago. Oops, I shouldn't have told you, but it's best to know these things upfront, don't you agree?"

Aaron, AKA Father Lawrence Burke, rambled on and on in his even, monotone voice.

"Your mother had another baby besides you, dear Blissy-Blissy. I wanted a boy, but sadly for me it was a girl. I would have taken him in and gotten a good price for the babe. Oh, Blissy, Blissy, what are we to do?"

She knew nothing about her mother giving up a baby. She wasn't so sure that he was *not* telling her the truth. Why would he lie to her about that? Unless he was totally insane.

To stay alive had been the only thing on her mind until now. The idea that her mother had had another baby took away what scant breath she had left. For a brief moment she felt numb, emotionless.

He continued, "And did I tell you that you're going to die in just a few minutes? Have patience. Decapitation, you know, takes time. All the tendons, arteries, bones ... that's a *lot* to hack through."

He paced in front of her. Seeing Bliss hanging, chained to the stark rocky wall, covered in blood-soaked linen, made him almost giddy. He noticed with approval that her knees had buckled.

He stepped toward her with the straight razor held tight in his right hand, next to his shoulder. He cocked his head and pulled his hand back to take the first long swipe.

She wasn't breathing. *Is she dead?* he wondered. *Perhaps she had suffocated or maybe bled to death. So sad. I wanted her alive when I removed her pretty little head. Oh, what's a man to do?*

Suddenly he saw a shadow in the flickering candlelight. He spun around fast, ready to charge.

CHAPTER THIRTY-TWO

5:19 PM Hawaii Time

As the jet dipped its wing for the final approach, Gordon could feel the adrenaline rush as his hands clutched the armrests. He thought about reaching for the barf bag, but decided to tough it out. His palms were sweating and his tired old heart pounded in anticipation of what was to come. He could see Diamond Head rise above the sandy beaches of Waikiki not far below.

The tires screeched and the tarmac smoked as the big jet touched down.

***

Kurt Gunderson leaned against a concrete pillar, relaxed with hands in his khaki pants. He wore a Hawaiian shirt under the pale blue sports coat and a cap with yellow lettering. In his right hand he massaged a long switchblade knife he had purchased earlier at a pawnshop in a seedy area east of Honolulu. He too, was anticipating things to come. He wore a thin smile as he watched the plane finally approaching the runway for its touchdown.

"Poppies? Poppies for you? One dollah each. Help a vet?"

"Get away from me, you fucking loser." Kurt grabbed the old thin black man by the shirt collar and pushed him hard, almost knocking him over the open-air railing to the lush garden twelve feet below.

The old man pushed himself away from the hard concrete railing and scooped up the red crepe-paper flowers that had fallen as he caught his breath. He picked up his black cap with the emblem of a lighting bolt through a red taro leaf, brushed it off before donning it again, and bowed slightly in Kurt's direction.

Kurt didn't like to be stared at. He didn't like crowded places either. The old man looked at him harmlessly. It bothered him, anyway.

Kurt took a step and grabbed at the old man again. As he did the man with the tattered shorts and Hawaiian shirt backed away, but Kurt got his cap in his hand and examined it.

"What the hell is this funny looking emblem on the front?" It looked like a red chile pepper. "You got a name?"

"Pila be my name," the old guy said.

Kurt glanced at the writing on the side of the bill of the black cap: 25th Infantry Division. "So, another goddamn homeless vet, huh? What's the matter with you? You got the fucking shakes, Pila? Afraid of your own shadow? Need a handout? I'll give you a handout." He cocked his arm, made a fist, and put it in motion.

Before he could lay it across the old man's jaw, a young man happened by and took action. He grabbed the cocked arm with one hand, and twisted it hard and fast behind his back, and forced him off-balance. Kurt banged up against the concrete pillar. The man grabbed Kurt's throat, pushed him sideways, bent him over the railing before turning him around to face him, and said, "You got a fight with this man, then, you got one with me, old man!"

Kurt Gunderson was clearly overpowered by a much younger and faster man. He was in uniform with a short-sleeved khaki shirt with red stripes on the side of his sleek blue pants, and spit-shined black leather shoes.

His eyes widened as the young man leaned in, almost touching Kurt's nose with his. With a handgrip on Kurt's throat so tight that his eyeballs seemed ready to pop, the marine said, "Touch this man again, and I'm going to twist your head in one direction until the only thing holding it on your shoulders will be your loose, ugly skin. And then, fuckhead, I'll just bite your head off! You got that, maggot?"

Kurt made a quick nod as snot oozed out of his nostrils.

The strong marine eased his grip, as he struggled to catch his breath. Then Kurt put both hands up to his red neck.

With a quick flick of his hand, the marine grabbed him again and flipped him over the rail to the rich floral display below.

Stepping back to the old vet, he asked if he was okay. Pila nodded, thanked him, and shook his hand saying, "Welcome home, brah."

He reached to the pavement and said, "I believe you dropped this." He picked up the hand-carved stick and handed it to the young marine. "Semper Fi," he said proudly.

The marine nodded, took the cane, and limped toward the open-air doorway. Pila noticed something else about the young marine. Not only did he have a limp, the sleeve on his left side was empty. No arm.

***

The ocean breeze was refreshing. Gordon took a deep breath and it felt good. No pains in his chest–a good omen, he felt. It gave him the courage to take charge. "M.G.," he said, "We're depending on you. We have to work fast. Use your cell phone, do your texting, whatever; you know the drill. Just stand ready."

M.G. half-listened as she thumbed her phone. "What are you going to do–you and Kat?"

Gordon was silent for a moment before replying, "I'm sending Kat back to Capitol City. She's getting three tickets for Hilo, on the Big Island."

"Perfect," she answered back. "I know that it's been a long day for you, but there's plenty of daylight left and we can use it. We'll need rentals. Get a Jeep. A two-door Wrangler, soft-top, for me. I don't care what you and Mick get."

"Okay," he said with a questioning look.

M.G. caught it. "We're going up to Volcano National Park, are we not? I may have to do some four-wheeling."

Gordon said, "They say it's a fifty-one minute flight, something like that. Mick's going to check in with his contacts here."

Mick smiled. He let Gordon act like he was in charge, as always. Regardless, Mick got the job done his way every time. Gordon got pissed about it, though he got over it eventually.

Kat was back to the crew with the tickets. "Guys," she said, "if you'll excuse us, Gordy and I are going to have a little chat."

She took Gordon's hand and led him to a rail over-looking a beautiful tropical garden. He leaned on it, waiting for Kat to talk first. He didn't have to wait long.

"Honey, listen. As much as I want to be here for you, and for the others, I have to go back. I checked my voice mail while waiting for the tickets and ... Chloe isn't handling things very well, it seems. I got a call from the hospital. She's causing quite a stir. She won't leave Maggie's body. Won't let anyone near her, in fact. She may have flipped out."

Gordon nodded, *he knew she had to go* and faked a frown. "You know best. I think it's wonderful you want to be there for Chloe ... and Maggie. The autopsy, funeral arrangements, it's a lot for Chloe to handle alone."

She nodded. "I'd be a hindrance to you guys, here."

His eyes watered and *that* was real. She dabbed them with her Kleenex. "You know I'll worry about you, too, Gordy."

As they turned to walk back to the others, a voice was heard behind them. "Poppies? Poppies for Veterans...."

They turned and saw the elderly black gentleman. Kat reached into her purse. Gordon held her arm still as he slipped the man a fin from his pocket, asking, "Your name?"

"Pila," he said with a smile and a nod. "My Hawaiian name. Thank you, sir. Mahalo."

A moment later, Gordon and Kat stepped up to Mick and M.G. "Kat's heading back to the hospital in Capital City," Gordon told them. "It seems that Chloe's come unglued."

***

As the Boeing 717 approached the airfield just outside of Hilo, Mickey had a question. "You two notice the skinny dude slipping into the men's room just as we walked past the cement pillar?"

M.G. nodded and so did Gordon.

"You mean the tall guy with a cap who looked like he'd been playing in the weeds with the red neck?" M.G. asked.

"I do," replied Mickey. "I wouldn't have thought twice about the guy, except that he actually had a red neck."

"Sunburn?" asked Gordon.

Nothing more was said.

The half-empty Hawaiian Airlines Boeing 717 touched down on the eastern side of the island. They exited the plane down the portable steps. After reaching the tarmac they were greeted by three men. They flashed their badges. FBI. Everyone walked inside.

"Any luggage?" one of them asked. There was no reply.

"Good. Come with us. I know a place where we can talk."

M.G. spoke up. "We may be followed." She was thinking of the red-necked guy back in Honolulu and Kurt Gunderson.

***

The same agent said, "It's safe. We'll talk as we go, if it's all right with you guys."

Once inside the sleek, black, Cadillac limo, they played Twenty Questions. As they played, M.G.'s thumbs were busy texting.

Inside Gordon's pants pocket, there was a sudden buzzing. As Mick's contacts were asking questions, Gordon checked his message.

dnt ask 4 wpns i got m krts twn ltr

He smiled as he put his phone back in his pocket. M.G. nudged him with her elbow.

Inside Chen's Chinese Kitchen, Mickey grabbed the menu and looked it over. He also looked over M.G.'s messages and two others before deciding what to eat.

The shorter agent with brown hair, who had been doing all the talking, introduced himself and the other two agents. Looking at each one of the mainlanders, he began. "Mick, Gordon, M.G., my name's Gunner. I work the Waikiki Beach district. Been on assignment here for two and a half years."

He looked to his tall blond partner. "This is Thomas J. Nachs. He's been here for two weeks now. He's going to be taking my place next week. I've been called back to Washington. And last but not least, is this old Hawaiian.

"He's lived here all his life. His Hawaiian name is too hard to remember, so he just tells *hoales* to call him Dano."

Mickey's eyebrows arched. "As in 'Book him, Dano?'" he asked, recalling *Hawaii Five O*.

Gunner grinned. "That's it. He's not exactly an agent–not officially anyway. He flies under the radar. One of those guys."

M.G. nodded, but said nothing as she reached and shook hands with them. After the introductions, they ate what Mickey ordered. Leave it to him to find the deal of the day, the Blue Plate Special.

It wasn't long before the $5.76 special was placed in front of them. The hot plate consisted of two scoops of rice, a choice of meat, one side, and a twenty-ounce drink.

"Fuck," Gunner muttered in amazement. "I've been here a hundred times, but I've never seen this on the menu."

Gordon smiled. "One thing about Mick, he doesn't miss a meal or a deal." Changing the subject, he asked, "Based on what you've heard from us and the reports, how many will it take to bring 'em down?"

Nachs looked to his mentor, Gunner, for an answer when Dano finally spoke up. "It's not about how many of us," he said, "it's about *them*. I know about the soldiers, and a little about the operation. We don't need an army. It's more of a matter of outsmarting them and taking out the leader or leaders. The foot soldiers will fold, some quicker than others. Then it becomes a matter of getting the innocent ones to safety.

"The soldiers are only in it for the money. The economy sucks here in Hawaii, ever since Dole pulled up stakes and fled to South America for cheaper labor."

Gunner dropped a Grant on the table as they left. He put a hand on Mickey's forearm, saying, "Nachs here is the new kid on the block. I think it'd be good for him to go along as an observer, to see how it works with you guys, of that's okay. You know what I mean?"

Mickey grunted. "As long as he's carrying a gat and can take direct orders, I've got no problem. He glanced at M.G. and Gordon. They shrugged as if to say okay.

"An FYI," Gunner said. "I've got a block of rooms set aside at the Hilo Hotel. It's on the bay. I'll be there. We're all set for daybreak tomorrow. We should surprise the hell out of 'em.

"And the seismologists say Volcano National Park is rumbling again and this time they expect a big shake any time. It could happen without warning. Scout it out and then get your asses back here. It'll be a long day tomorrow."

***

As arranged by Mick's contacts, the rentals were awaiting them in Chen's parking lot. "Follow me to Kurtistown, boys. "They're waiting for me." M.G.climbed into her two-door Jeep Wrangler. The others followed behind in the rented Chrysler Sebring convertible. They turned off the one hundred block of East Puainaki Street, and onto Highway 11, heading south toward the angry volcano goddess, Madam Pele.

Mick checked his watch before pulling out of the parking lot. "It's almost seven, guys. What's our ETA?"

Dano answered, "It's thirty miles from here. The sun will be setting sometime after we arrive at the main entrance. No biggie, though. Full moon, plenty of lights, and lots of activity. They're evacuating the campers tonight. I imagine there'll be buses, mini-vans, all that."

"Chaos?" Mick questioned.

"Could be," Dano said. "What do you have in mind?"

Mick glanced to his partner, Gordon.

Dano said, "We'll be in Kurtistown soon."

CHAPTER THIRTY-THREE

7:01 PM – The Death Caves

"Aaron!" yelled Lilia. "Have you gone mad?" No sooner did she speak than the ground rocked and rolled. Small chunks of rocks fell from the ceiling of the den. Cracks grew along the floor, and steam hissed from the tiny fissures.

He dropped the straight razor and erupted in a strange cackling laugh. Exhausted, dripping with blood and sweat, he stumbled to the chair behind the desk and collapsed.

Hours ago she sensed that his mind was going south. Now it was shattered. She decided to take charge.

The sulphur stung her eyes and throat. "Aaron," she said as her eyes began to water, "Lio is getting the other guards to gather the two groups separately. I've got a school bus topside as close to the back entrance as we can get it. It should be here within the hour, if it's not here already."

Aaron said nothing. He just sat there breathing unsteadily, alternately coughing and giggling. She glanced over to Bliss, chained and unconscious.

Lio materialized at the entrance to the den.

"Ms. Lilia, I've got Lawai'a and three others with the midwives. My three are with the pregnant ones and the babies. The *haole* breeders are with them, too."

In the shadows, he saw Bliss. The sight of her, covered in blood and seemingly lifeless, took his breath away. Then he thought he detected some movement—a twitch of her head. Or had he imagined it? He scanned the small room to the figure at the desk. He stared for a moment before turning to Lilia.

"Yes, Lio. This is the situation. Direct the breeders to me. I'll have them take her topside to the dumpster."

"No! Too dangerous topside, I can have my soldiers take her to the death caves."

"Good idea, Lio. Fetch the two *haoles* and bring them to me. Check to see if our bus is here. If so, take the babies and the pregnant ones only."

"And the midwives?" Lio asked.

"Only if there's time," she snapped.

Lio was gone in a flash. Lilia found the key to the wrist cuffs and unlocked one wrist at a time. It wasn't easy, but moving dead weight never is. Bliss's body collapsed to the floor in a heap.

Lilia, now too, covered in blood, stepped to the front of the desk, where Aaron sat mumbling and bleeding.

"We can't stay here any longer," she said. "The caves are too dangerous. We've already lost our lead soldier, Luna. Many of the midwives and some of the pregnant ones have been injured. We don't have much time. The sky is falling, Aaron. The sulphur dioxide is getting to all of us. Do you understand?"

"Shoot me up! Shoot me up!"

Lilia sighed, opened a drawer at the desk, and pulled out a full syringe. She plunged it deep into a vein in Aaron's left forearm. The heroin took possession of him immediately. He slumped back in the chair, his arms limp at his side, dripping crimson droplets to the floor.

***

Somewhere in the subconscious depths of Bliss's mind a voice spoke: *"Breathe, dear precious one. You are loved, dear heart."*

All at once the body gasped for air. Still crumpled on the warm, hard floor, she gasped again and again. Too weak to speak, her lips moved without a sound. "Mom. Never give up! Never give up. Help me, spirit...." Her throat and eyes burned. She stopped breathing again.

***

At the park entrance near the back of a brick rest area building, Lio popped his head up behind a large lava rock with thick brush in front of it. He could smell the diesel fuel as the yellow school bus' engine idled.

The middle-aged *haole* driver inside was thumbing through a free-bie tourist magazine. Lio stepped to the door and tapped on it. The driver reached for the door lever and opened the bus door.

"We'll be loading soon," he said. The driver nodded and Lio turned and ducked around the bushes. As he did, he came face to face with Kurt Gunderson.

With his cap pulled low over his forehead, Kurt smiled as he ambled up and pulled his knife up to Lio's nose. "Don't say a word. Take me to your boss."

Lio froze for a second. He recognized this guy from a recent encounter. He didn't like him. Lio put a hand on Kurt's forearm and pushed it aside as he stepped below the lava rock and ducked down and out of sight. Kurt followed.

An old beat-up red '71 Datsun B210 was parked on the other side of the brick outhouse. Inside, an older black gentleman watched and chuckled.

CHAPTER THIRTY-FOUR

11:11 PM CST

B ack at Lutheran Hospital in Capital City, Chloe sat guarding
Maggie's body. It was quiet in the small room. She'd been there
a while and had nodded off. In her dream, she was coming out of another crazy dream. She saw herself opening her eyes. When she did,
her attention was seized by something strange; for a brief moment, she
thought she could see the sheet move, almost imperceptibly. It was as
if Maggie was breathing again.

Suddenly, Maggie's body heaved, as she made a throaty gasping
sound. Startled, Chloe jumped for the door and ran into the hallway. A
young hospital chaplain dressed in a black jacket and white collar was
passing by. They collided.

She stood in front of him in shock and said, "I'll be a son of a
bitch!"

Taken aback, he said, "I beg your pardon?"

It was then that the two aides in white, standing on either side of
the door grabbed her and took her to the other end of the hall. As they
waited for the elevator she glanced back. She saw a local undertaker
take Maggie out of the room on a hospital gurney. Chloe screamed.

The men in white took her to the fourth floor and placed her in a
padded room.

One aide turned to the other and said, "Glad that's over with. That
woman is nuts!"

CHAPTER THIRTY-FIVE

7:22 PM - The Big Island

L ilia stood silent, observing the situation.
She raised her voice: *"Aaron ... Aaron!"*

His eyes rolled. He squinted as he looked from
Lilia and back to Bliss lying on the floor.

"They're here, Aaron. Your friend Kurt, as well as that group from the seminary. They just landed. Are there any instructions?"

He teetered unsteadily on the chair from side to side. He breathed hard and long, his arms shaking. Aaron was exhausted; his eyes rolled until only the whites showed. Blood continued dripping to the floor from his upper body.

Lilia looked at him then turned to the lifeless body of the young woman on the warm, almost hot floor.

The noxious odor steamed through several fissures from the ground below as the room began to shake again. The tremors were more severe. The floor heaved upward and stayed that way.

Out of a steaming fissure near the entrance to the den, molten magma oozed up and out. The red-hot flowing magma crept toward the desk where Aaron sat in a drug-induced stupor.

***

Lio had made his way to the young pregnant teens with their babies. He instructed his guards to take them to the back entrance and load them onto the bus.

The entire chain of lava tubes was rumbling and shaking as heavy steam poured through the floors and walls.

"Wiki wiki!" he said. "We don't have much time. The volcano is about to erupt!"

They were almost a half mile south of the National Volcano Visitor Center, deep under the Halema'uma'u Trail. It was going to take time to get the young women and the babies out. *"Wiki,* let's go!"

Under a cot he saw movement. Lio stepped to it and kicked at it. One of the frightened breeders scrambled to his feet. "Lilia has ordered you and your friend to her den," Lio screamed at him. "Go now!" The two scampered out of the den and disappeared down the narrow, winding, steaming tube.

CHAPTER THIRTY-SIX

A t the side of the road just outside of Kurtistown, a scruffy guy in his mid-twenties handed M.G. a heavy canvas bag. She in turn handed him a thick wad of one hundred dollar bills.

Parked behind her in the Sebring convertible were Mick, Gordon, Dano, and his newbie charge, Thomas J. Nachs.

Gordon observed the transaction and told Nachs, "Get up there with M.G. Help her divvy things up. Shake a leg."

In a jiffy Nachs was in the passenger seat with M.G. and separating the fully loaded, semi-automatic Glock .357 SIG and a hundred clips of ammo. He made two trips back to their car.

"M.G. wants me to go with her," Nachs told Mickey, adding with a patronizing grin, "says she'll teach me a thing or two. Oh, something else: she said to tell you that Kurt Gunderson was on the road here not long ago. He thinks he's being followed. Not sure on that one, but that's what the guy with the guns said, anyway.

"Yeah, go with M.G.," Mickey told him. "Somehow she seems to know the exact spot of the entrance to the lava tubes."

Gordon and Mick made eye contact as the lead car took to the road again.

Dano had the backseat to himself. In a quiet voice he said, "You guys knew Richard Fleming, I take it." He saw their eyes glued to the rearview mirror, staring back at him. "I knew him, too. I used his

199

services once. I took him golfing at Makalei Golf Club. It's just up the hill from the Kona Airport on the other side of the island."

They listened but said nothing. He rattled on about his service. He'd apparently had been involved in covert ops for some time, most of it in Hawaii, including forays to the Philippines, Fiji, and Guam.

Gordon finally had a question. "Dano, what's your name?"

He looked to the rearview mirror, knowing they'd have their eyes on him as he spoke. "Kane-hekili Mākaha."

Mickey glanced over to Gordon who looked straight ahead. Kane-hekili Mākaha looked back to the mirror and said, "But, hey, feel free to call me Dano."

"Mick," Gordon said, "Flick the brights on M.G. We have to pull over."

Off the side of the road, they huddled on the passenger side of her Jeep. "According to Gunner and the map here, the Visitor Center is located between mile marker 30 and 31. The place closed at five, so we'll ditch the car near the gate if it's locked. M.G., you get to four-wheel."

She beamed as she took a look at her cell phone. "It's getting exciting, boys." She put the phone down and nodded. "There's little daylight left and we've got things to do."

Vans, cars and minibuses passed through the open gate, coming and going. M.G. parked her Jeep away from the Center, next to a yellow school bus parked near a red brick toilet. They all piled out.

Gordon had to relieve himself. He walked to the brick building toward the door marked, MEN. As he stood in front of the urinal emptying his bladder, he made a guttural sound, "Ah."

A figure materialized next to him. "Hey, you old snake-in-the-grass."

Gordon jumped, his urine stream going wild for a moment. He got it under control and started zipping up.

"Jesus, William, you scared the *piss* out of me! What's the matter with you." He flushed and turned to face the dark stranger. "I'm sorry, I thought you were–"

The older black gentleman gave him a bewildered look.

"Sorry, I thought you were someone else," Gordon said. "It's been a long day." He flushed and walked to the sink as the old man flushed.

Gordon looked at the mirror and said, "Hey, You're the guy with the poppies at the airport. You called me a snake-in-the-grass. That's why I thought you were someone else. Why'd you call me that?"

"I'm sorry, I thought you were someone else, too," the man said after a pause. He flushed and added, "My Hawaiian name is Pila."

Back in the parking lot M.G. was out of her Jeep, standing with Nachs and the others. She wrinkled her nose and said, "That sulphur smell is *potent*, man." Her eyes were watering like crazy.

The rest agreed. The stench bothered everybody. There was so much steaming sulpher coming from the ground, it was as if the whole place was in a dense cloud. Then the ground shook again as a loud speaker crackled from the main building.

"We urge everyone to leave the area now! Please gather your belongings and head north to Hilo. It's the safest route. Don't panic, but be speedy. Mahalo!"

"Alrighty then," M.G. said to no one in particular.

Gordon emerged from the men's room doorway, followed by his new acquaintance. They stepped toward the old faded Datsun. Mick saw them and followed with the others behind.

Pila was talking as Gordon listened. When the others joined them, Gordon introduced him to the others.

"This guy's name is Pila," Gordon told them. "Turns out he had a run-in with Gunderson at the Honolulu airport." He introduced him to Mick and the others as Nachs leaned against the old man's car and pulled a cigarette from his shirt pocket and lit it.

"He happens to be a guide. He's an old hand at spelunking. He says he knows his way around the lava tubes here."

Dano eyed him up and down and said, "How do you know the lava tubes here? Unless you worked for the park, no one, and I mean *no one* is allowed in those tubes. It's too damned dangerous."

The others agreed. They were waiting for a plausible answer from the old man. What remained unsaid, though they were too reluctant to say aloud, was that the old vet looked far too old to be rummaging around in collapsing lava tubes.

CHAPTER THIRTY-SEVEN

7:28 PM - Decisions

"**A**ll I can tell you is this, folks ..." Pila said as he walked around to the other side of his Datsun. "Time is of the essence. I followed you guys and Kurt Gunderson right to this very spot. Not at the same time, but you get my drift. I know where he went," he said, pointing to the other side of the brick building.

Dano eyed the others for a few seconds before saying, "What are we waiting for? Let's move!"

"Wait," Mick said, putting his hand up, "let's hear the old guy out." He shot a look to Dano, then back to Gordon.

Pila continued as he doffed his cap and wiped his forehead. "I got a hunch that if you just stand back and observe for a few moments, your job, whatever that is, will be a lot easier." He pointed to the yellow school bus. "The engine is running and a driver is at the wheel. He's waiting for somebody or something, ya?"

Dano started a side conversation with M.G., expressing his doubts about this character. "Dano," Mick interrupted, "let's hear him out, okay?" He didn't shoot a glance at Dano this time; he stared at him.

Pila shook his head and said, "Hey, like I say, I'm just a guide."

He nodded to the group and stepped toward the Visitors Center, fading into the hazy mist formed from the newly erupting fissures of steam.

Dano seemed confused. "You guys aren't seriously listening to that old coot, are you?"

Gordon looked at the others before speaking. "I for one think he's right—right about the bus, anyway. And if, I say *if,* he's right, we'll know it by who gets on the damn bus."

Nachs agreed with Dano's reasoning, but he was willing to go along with whatever the group decided.

Mick had to have his say. "If my old sidekick thinks we should wait, as the old man said, then I say we wait."

"Hold on a minute," Gordon said. "I thought you were *my* sidekick..."

Mick ignored him. "Hell, we don't even know where to start looking, do we? I mean about an entrance to the web of lava tubes. Do you, Dano? M.G., what about your contacts? They say anything about that?"

Before she could answer, there was a noise from the bus, a pneumatic wheezing sound as the driver pulled a lever to open the side door. They all huddled on the far side of Pila's car to get a better look.

They watched as a tall, strong and shirtless Hawaiian appeared at the door, a holstered handgun hanging at his waist. He seemed to be giving the driver instructions. He then took a step toward the door with one arm outstretched. A second later he pulled a young woman forward and helped her get aboard the bus.

Another shirtless man appeared as the first one jumped off the bus and disappeared around the big bush in front of it. This second guy was as tall as the first Hawaiian, but bigger and wider.

M.G. whispered to the others. "That girl. She looks pregnant—*very* pregnant."

They watched as the young woman waddled to the back of the bus and took a seat. Other pregnant women followed, some carrying infants. Soon the bus was full of young mothers and their babies. Just before the door closed, the big man stood by the driver, waving a revolver around.

"Sonofabitch," Nachs said, amazed that the old man had been right all along.

With a sudden jolt, the ground began to rock and roll. It shook everyone in the vicinity of the Visitor Center. Panic had set in. People screamed as they ran for safety. Tires squealed on the blacktop as vehicles of all kinds sped out of the parking lot, down the road past the entrance, and onto the highway below.

"Dano," Mick said, "Call Gunner, ASAP. Have him arrange an escort for that bus. Tell him to stop it and get that goddamned gunman off it! Then call the local police. We got a situation here."

Dano flipped open his cell and began his call. M.G. was already busily moving her thumbs around hers.

Mick glanced at Gordon before blurting out, "Someone's gotta follow that bus!"

A figure materialized from behind Gordon. "I'll follow it," Pila announced, and hurried back to his car.

As the bus backed out of the parking stall, the group slipped back into the shadow of the building, watching the bus creep toward the entrance in line with the other vehicles. The old red Datsun was just one vehicle behind it, followed by others forming a convoy, all leaving in a state of panic.

"Follow me," Gordon said, as he ducked behind the building. They followed him to the large lava rock mostly hidden from view by thick shrubbery.

"The bus was in front of this bush." Gordon said, looking puzzled.

Mickey asked, "And?"

"And all those women came from this direction," Dano answered. "But from where, exactly?" He stepped ahead of the rest, and flashed a light as he pushed aside a large, leafy branch. "Look," he said. "The entrance is down there."

He went first into the narrow crevice, followed by Nachs, then M.G., Mickey, and Gordon pulled up the rear. Once inside they were surprised that there was a dim light in the space and it stretched downward along a narrow footpath.

Mick shook his head. "I gotta ask, Gordy. How could you trust a guy you just met in the john?"

Gordon shrugged. "Seemed like a good omen. He called me a snake-in-the-grass. Only one other person ever called me that. William."

"What's the plan, now?" M.G. asked as she pulled out her Glock .357 SIG from its holster.

CHAPTER THIRTY-EIGHT

7:47 PM - Magma

On the mainland there is fog. In the cities, it's smog. Here on a volcano it's called vog, and the air topside was thick with it. Without a breeze from the ocean, it became more difficult to breathe. But it was worse, far worse, underground.

As Gordon coughed, Mickey took control. "Okay, everyone check their weapons. Safety on or off? Check it. We go single file. Keep at least ten feet apart. Be quiet and listen for movement ahead. Try to stay in step. M.G., ready to lead the way?"

"Yup," she said in a hushed voice.

"Good," Mickey said. "I'll be behind you, followed by Nachs, Dano, and Gordon." There was a deep rumbling underfoot. It was hard just to keep their balance. The smell was gross as they made their way through the hissing tube, but the fear was worse, not knowing what they were in for.

A few minutes into the tube they were approaching a diagonal intersection. M.G. put her hand up.

They stopped at once. She heard voices coming from a distance. She took a breath and held it. Hugging the wall with her back pressed against it, she leaned and looked to her left down the long tube. She saw nothing.

Exhaling, she ducked back in line with the others. One voice ahead became louder. They could hear it. There was another quick, angry shake. Pieces of rock fell away from the top of the tube.

Dust filled the thick air. Gordon coughed, quickly putting an arm to his mouth to muffle the sound. He coughed again and again. The lights flicked once, then went out.

"Uh-oh," someone said. They stayed quiet. No one spoke.

A moment later they noticed a flicker of light coming from the other tube. Again, M.G. slowly poked her head around the corner, looking upward to her right where the light was coming from. Someone was lighting lanterns.

"It's coming from up that way, to the right," she whispered to the others. "It's roughly two hundred feet or so. It's a room or something at the end of the tunnel, maybe."

"Can you see anyone there?" Mick asked.

"Just shadows," she replied. "What do we do, boss?"

"We wait," he said. "In the meantime, we think. What's down here? Who's down here? How many guards? Like that."

M.G. thought a second. "Didn't Bliss say something about midwives?"

"Yeah, she did," Mick whispered. "How many, you think? A dozen?"

"Or less," she said. "How many do you think for the ones we saw on the bus?"

No one answered. M.G. put a finger to her lips and squatted low. The others did the same. From down in the other tube M.G. thought she could hear footsteps. She saw a light flicker from the distance. The light got brighter as the footsteps became louder.

Everyone stepped back. Crouching in the darkness, they remained silent. Gordon could feel the tickle in his throat again. This time, though, pains in his chest accompanied the tickle. His eyes watered as he tried to hold the cough back, almost gagging. The light and shadows passed by quickly. Gordon turned and felt his way back up the tube, until he felt he reached a safe distance, before putting an arm to his mouth and coughing.

***

As Lio and Kurt reached the vog-filled room, Lio stopped dead in his tracks at the entrance. The oozing magma on the floor gave off steam as it inched forward. He looked to Lilia.

"We have to leave, Lio," she said, "the four of us–you, the breeders, and me. They can help us." She clasped a hand over her mouth. "God, the fumes. The heat. It's too much."

Lio shot a look to the two men. He looked back to Lilia and understood.

Kurt stepped around them, hugging the wall as he made his way to the front of the desk where Aaron sat. He eyed his boss, glanced to Lilia then Lio, and looked back to Aaron.

He reached into a pocket and pulled something out. Then he held it in front of Aaron, who looked up at the closed hand. Kurt opened it, exposing the two gold fillings, each with a tiny GPS chip and a single microchip. Aaron frowned as Kurt dropped two metal pieces on the desk saying, "These came from Richard Fleming." He dropped the other and said, "This, from the bitch at the seminary."

With glassy eyes, Aaron stared at the objects on the desk. He shook his head and said, "You fool, Kurt. You utter fool."

Not far underground there was another tremendous shake, the worst one yet. The walls shifted dangerously as the floors heaved upward, sending large rocks from the ceiling to smash to the hot floor below. Plumes of dust and debris quickly filled the tubes. Breathing was almost impossible.

Lio became wild-eyed with alarm and looked ready to bolt. "Come, Lilia," he shouted. "We must leave now!" He stepped in and grabbed her arm. The breeders tiptoed behind her, terrified of the molten magma that came closer to their feet. "Hurry, it isn't safe here any longer," Lio cried. "If we stay we'll be crushed."

As they stepped over the debris, they trekked down the pitch-black tube as Lio held out the lantern in front of them. They stopped cold at the corridor where the others were; their path was blocked by fallen rocks. They edged around it as Lio spoke: "We must go now! There's no time. I know another way out...."

Lilia stumbled, twisting her ankle. "Damn it!" she said, wincing in pain. She leaned against the wall as she massaged the soreness.

It gave her time to think about Lawai'a and the other guards. She dismissed the midwives. To her they were just extra baggage. "Lio," she said, "it's just us now. We've got to get to that ship that's anchored at the front of the hotel in Hilo Bay."

Lio helped her to her feet. "What about Lawai'a and the other guards?" He glanced back with a panicked look and said, "And your *haole*, Aaron, the woman Bliss, and that guy, Kurt. What about them?"

"What *about* them?" she snorted as she pushed him forward. She read the fear and uncertainty on his face and said, "They, too, have become excess baggage. You and me, Lio, we'll be on that ship and gone, far away from here. You'll be rich, Lio, rich beyond your wildest dreams. I'll treat you right, don't worry about that."

The four moved down the corridor toward the old communications center, heading for the death caves, to safety.

Deep within the lava tube at the opening to the death caves, desperate voices were heard. "Let's dig!" someone shouted and they began lifting and moving the heavy rubble.

***

Back in the end room, Aaron sat facing Kurt as shadows from the flickering oil lamps danced on the walls.

"Your job is finished then, Mr. Gunderson?"

Kurt nodded, saying, "Per your instructions, sir. And may I say I had tremendous fun doing away with the women at the seminary. The final one, that Margaret Lynne, was pure delight." Kurt smiled like a boy on Christmas morning.

A green aura appeared in the vog-filled room where the body lay. It became brighter and brighter, before turning a burnt orange color.

The body seemed to move. Suddenly, there was an eerie change. From the body a female spirit arose. Fire shot through her eyes. With a hot colored bandana across her forehead, her hair was long, half-braided, half-flowing and aloft, looking almost like wings.

One of her eyes was a vibrant brown, the other a fire-flecked blue, as streams of colors shot from her right eye to the entrance of the room. Around her neck she wore a metallic rainbow-colored necklace with a gleaming multi-colored pendant with an elongated stone. From it, hot fire shot forward as her colored eyes peered through Aaron and Kurt.

She was an angel, an avenging angel. Arms outstretched, they became wing-like as she arched toward the two men. Aaron numbly stood as the blood leaked from his ashen body. Kurt pulled a knife and was ready to take her down.

Leaning next to him, she opened her mouth and countless thousands of fiery white maggots flew out, engulfing him.

Howling and with arms flailing about, he stumbled as he tried to run, and bumped his head on a hanging kerosene lantern, shattering the glass.

In an instant, he was engulfed in flames. Screaming, he stumbled forward, stepping into the molten ooze in the middle of the floor. Sheer agony held him pinned to the spot. His screams turned to blood-curdling howls as the flowing magma pulled him downward. He was crazy with pain, shrieking like a banshee as his outstretched arms crackled in the blaze. His screams echoed throughout the veins of the lava tubes while he melted into the fiery, rolling magma.

***

Nachs was the first one out. He scrambled into the other lava tube. One by one he helped the others enter the other vein. They stared at the ball of flames at the end of the tube.

CHAPTER THIRTY-NINE

In the Death Caves

G ordon was working hard just to breathe.

"Dano, you come with us," Mick said as he opened a small leather pouch attached to his belt. He pulled a small flashlight from it.

Coughing, Gordon took a quick look at M.G., then to Mick and said, "I'll take M.G. with me up to the fire and see what's there, then we'll catch up."

Nachs and Dano followed Mick as he headed down the tube where the others had gone.

M.G. took Gordon's hand as she led the way to the end of the dark, voggy tube. Gordon stumbled but kept up. For a man his age, he told himself for encouragement, he did all right. Then it happened. There was another scream from the room, only this time it was a very different kind of scream-one of horrifying awareness. It made Gordon think of the terror of a cornered animal about to become prey to a hungry coyote.

***

Now the avenging angel turned her attention to Aaron.

She hovered over the desk as he stood with his back to the far wall, screaming as he looked to his burning right hand.

The angel spoke. Her voice was soft and surprisingly clear considering the chaos all around them. "You shouldn't have touched those children," she said. Then a half-smile lit her face with a beatific glow. "Toasty in here, isn't it?"

Beams of fire shot from her eyes directly to his left hand this time. He screamed bloody murder. Both hands were now on fire, the flames moving up his flailing arms. He screamed louder as the red-orange flames licked his flesh, moving closer to his head.

She looked to the floor where he stood. Jets of flame shot from her eyes to his bare feet; they too were set ablaze. The avenger watched for a few long seconds as the delirious man jumped about, screaming and wailing in agony. She opened her mouth again. A stream of white light engulfed the entire flaming body of Lawrence Burke.

"It's hell, ain't it?" she said with a chuckle as she watched him writhe and collapse to the floor, screaming the final screams of his life.

Flames shot to the ceiling. She looked again to the woman on the floor and floated to her. The angel then turned to M.G. and Gordon as they stood near the entrance watching. She opened her mouth.

M.G. clung to Gordon. For the first time in a long, long time she was truly frightened. Their eyes were glued to the apparition as a metal object appeared far back in her throat. It shot out of her mouth and pitched forward. Gordon reflexively raised a hand and caught it. The small piece of metal scorched his palm, and he tossed it like a hot potato from one hand to the other.

All the while the spirit gazed at Gordon. Her eyes shifted to the long narrow lava tube, and then back to him. She made a slight nod then faded back into the lifeless body on the floor–and she was gone.

M.G. and Gordon stood at the entrance, unable to budge for a long moment. Then they snapped to, looked down at the rolling magma and stepped quickly toward Bliss.

M.G. put two fingers just below her left ear.

"Goddam, there's a pulse!" she said in surprise.

They managed to get her between them. As they did, the lights blinked once and stayed on. Together they gently moved Bliss out of the room and down the tube toward the back entrance where they came in.

Midway Gordon grunted, "Wait..." They stopped. He had to catch his breath. Almost as an afterthought he handed the metal object to M.G. She looked at it.

"A key?" she asked.

He clutched his chest saying, "Did you understand what she said?"

M.G.'s eyes widened. "You heard her, too? I thought I'd imagined it."

"Get one of the others to help you with the midwives. Tell Mick to be on the alert. You know why, right?"

"I do," she said. "Be careful, Gordon, please."

***

Lio, Lilia, and the breeders moved through the communications section and made their way closer to the site of the death caves. They stopped. Lio put the lantern down as the lights flickered. "Damn," he muttered.

The lower end of the lava tube's ceiling had collapsed, and ahead of them lay an impassable wall of rocks. There was a small beam of light at the top and to the side of the rubble. Carefully Lio went forward, moving rocks as he ascended. One by one he pushed them aside, until he slipped out of sight.

Raymond and Darrell turned to Lilia, fear etched in their eyes.

She smirked and said, "Relax, boys, Lio knows what he's doing. He's a *man*. What the fuck are you guys?"

Lio reappeared, sticking his head out from behind the rubble and looking down at them. "There's a way out. I don't like it, but we have no other choice." From a distance, they heard voices. *"Wiki wiki,"* Lio shouted, urging them to be quick about it. "This way!" He held out a hand and shouted, "Hurry!"

***

M.G. had caught up with the others and told them about Bliss and Gordon. She also told them that Aaron and Kurt had burned to death. That was all she told them, except that she had a key.

They were standing at the edge of the pile of fallen lava rocks, behind which they could hear the women's voices. Using their bare hands, they dug into the piles of rocks as fast as they could. A grasping hand appeared from the rubble on the other side. They moved the debris away and pulled the woman to safety.

"The others," she panted, "are still in chains." Breathing hard, she collapsed in Nach's arms.

Once inside, they found the women and M.G. unlocked their wrist bracelets, freeing them. They were weak, malnourished, disoriented, in shock, and had numerous cuts and multiple injuries.

Dano checked the ceiling. "Hey," he called, "there's an air hole here." He took a step onto a nearby cot and jumped with his arms high until he grabbed and held onto the edge of the hole.

With his head poking into the upper level he looked around, seeing nothing but lava rocks and small bushes. He let go of the edge and landed on the floor below.

"If we can get 'em up there, we can get 'em out, yeah?" Dano asked.

Nachs spotted a crude wooden ladder on the floor. "There's our answer, guys."

"Great!" Mick said, "Take 'em up. All of 'em, Nachs. Secure the area and call for assistance."

M.G. scanned the room. She stepped toward the woman whom they had first encountered. She asked, "Were you ladies guarded?"

"Always," the woman replied. "Lawai'a was the main one, the one they called the Fisherman. When the last shake came, the three other guards came and begged him to leave. They were as scared as we were. He went with them, leaving us in chains like you found us. We thought we would die here." The woman burst into sobs and embraced M.G. in gratitude.

"You're safe now," M.G. whispered to her. "Help is on the way. Stay with Nachs here, okay? He's a good guy."

He set the ladder up to the air hole. At long last, one by one, the women began their ascent to freedom.

M.G., Mick, and Dano trotted along the narrow winding tube, following the many footprints left in the thick mud that covered the floor. Fissures hissed and groundwater dripped in all around them as they made their way into the communications chamber. There they stopped to catch their breath.

Looking at the countless folders strewn about the place, the toppled phones and computers, Mickey saw something odd. "Damn." It was the leg of a man sticking out of the rubble. The falling ceiling had crushed the body. He saw M.G. staring down the tunnel. "You're right, M.G." He led the way, M.G. behind him, followed by Dano.

As they were about to round the next bend, Mickey stopped, as did the other two. They stood silent as he lowered himself. Moving forward as he crouched, he stopped again and put a hand up.

He turned and whispered, "I see three of them. Two men, one woman. They're climbing rocks. It looks like there was a cave-in down there."

M.G. looked to Mick, as did Dano. With guns drawn, they were ready for action. They watched as someone else materialized at the top of the rock pile near the ceiling. He seemed to be pulling the others upward.

"That's four," M.G. said. "How many more *are* there?"

No sooner did she ask when there was more movement near the ceiling. They watched the others step back, looking up at the figure.

CHAPTER FORTY

Inside the Death Chamber

L awai'a crawled half out of the hole and said, "Lio, I see a way out through dese death caves. It's amazing! Come! *Wiki wiki!*"

Lio stared up at Lawai'a. "Where da others? Gone, ya?"

Lawai'a pointed downward. Lilia and Lio looked closer at the pile of rocks. Raymond jumped back as several rocks rolled down, exposing an arm.

Lio removed more of the rubble exposing the crushed head of another guard. He stopped and looked up to Lawai'a, who nodded sadly.

"Like dat. All six of 'em," he said. "They help me up here, da big shake come. Madam Pele plenty angry, no? We go now. Come, we blow dis joint, ya?"

He reached a hand down. Lilia looked to Lio, then he helped her up the rocks to grab Lawai'a's helping hand.

Mick turned to the others. "Let's do it."

"No," Dano replied. "I'm afraid the gunfire could trigger another ceiling collapse."

The three crouched shoulder-to-shoulder, waiting as they watched the others move up the rocks.

"Okay, but just one shot," Dano said, "from here." He put both hands on the revolver, flipped the safety and squeezed off a round. The noise was thunderous, echoing and vibrated throughout the tubes.

Raymond Polanski's body lurched. He turned to Lilia with a look of complete surprise.

Then he looked down the front of his dirty white shirt. Blood spewed from his chest. He fell to his knees as he brought his hands to his gaping wound.

His eyes rolled and he fell forward onto the rocks in front of him.

Mick, M.G., and Dano lay flat on the muddy floor of the tube as Lio returned fire. Several rounds glanced off the walls, ceiling and floor.

"Oomph!" M.G. felt a searing pain. A bullet had struck her left leg, just below her calf muscle.

Mickey and Dano felt pain, too. Flying chips of rock, and shrapnel from the bullets grazed their outstretched arms and shoulders.

***

Lilia had been pulled through the hole near the ceiling. It was Lio's turn. He climbed up fast, like a monkey.

As Mick and Dano let loose with their Glocks, he dove through the hole, barely escaping the hail of bullets.

***

A faint, high-pitched scream was heard from the rock pile. Raymond Polanski was hit again. This time he took a bullet to his groin. As he writhed in agony, an apparition appeared before him and whispered:

"My dear Raymond. This is not the end for you. It is the beginning! You must atone for your sins. Soon you will feel the pain of all of your innocent young victims and their families...."

Raymond Polanski's contorted face froze in time as the blood drained from his lifeless body.

***

M.G. cut and tore away a part of her jeans from the right foot to her knee, and wrapped it around her wound. "Nothing's broken, guys," she said. "The bullet must have passed through."

Bleeding, the three of them jumped to their feet. With guns aimed at the hole near the ceiling, they ran single file toward the heap of rocks, expecting more gunfire.

***

Lawai'a was already at the back of the first chamber.

"Over here," he said as he held a lantern in front of him.

Lilia, Lio, and Darrell ran to him.

"Look. There," he said, pointing the lantern to the doorway behind him.

"Oh, God!" Lilia said. Resting on both sides of the golden doorway were two skeletons, each wearing leis made of seashells. A braided wreath sat perched atop their skulls. One skeletal hand held a spear adorned with ornate gems and braided reeds.

"They are guards from long ago," Lio explained. "Those two were assigned to guard this passageway to the death chambers of our ancestors. Beyond, in the next chamber, should be the ones who came to these islands thousands of years ago. They were the first to arrive here from Tahiti and beyond."

"Let's go, Lio," the fisherman said. "The others are close behind.

When Lio didn't move from his spot, Lawai'a turned and said, "What's the matter with you? You weren't afraid before, Lio."

Lawai'a was right. He wasn't afraid then, but now everything was different. He was invading a sacred place, the final resting ground of the souls of valor and pride. Lio knew he shared none of those qualities and entering this place would be taboo. He hesitated.

A shot rang out from the other end of the chamber. It smacked into the wall, just missing Lilia. They all ran deep into the darkness of the guarded chamber, not knowing or even thinking about what to expect.

***

Dano climbed through the small entrance above the rocks first and held a hand out to M.G. She limped up over the rocks, made her way through, and followed Dano into the chamber. Mick followed after her. They crouched low, and as he pointed his flashlight, they ran to the other end and stopped.

Standing to one side of the open doorway, M.G. felt something dangerously sharp touching her backside. "Mick," she gasped fearfully, "shine your light over here." When he did, he almost shouted aloud. "Jesus, it's a–"

"Ssh!" Dano hushed him.

M.G. turned her head slowly and gasped at the skeletal remains of an ancient guard. The tip of his spear was touching her butt. She edged away.

"Yeah, this must be the entrance to a sacred death cave," Dano said. "Legend has it that our ancestors were buried in lava tubes. I've never seen them. Never set foot in sacred burial grounds before. It was all just folklore as far as I knew."

Mick cocked his head and said, "It's time to find out."

Dano paused. Beads of sweat formed on him. He took a breath and let it out. "Be my guest," he said. "I led you here. Guess I'll follow you now."

Mick leaned toward the doorway. Lilia and Lio let loose with their side arms. Some of the bullets slammed into the wall. The rest whizzed through the doorway.

"Shit!" Mickey said. "I hate gunfire." He poked his arm through the doorway and pulled the trigger several times. M.G. did the same, firing off five rounds.

Leaning back against the wall, they prepared for return fire. There was none. They reloaded, catching their breath. There was a commotion in the next room. Shots were fired and screams were heard.

Mick turned to M.G., then to Dano. Looking to him, Mick shrugged.

Dano cocked his head. "I don't know. What do you guys think?"

Mick shrugged again. He crouched and took a quick look inside. Turning back he said, "All I can see is a dim light near the floor. A lantern." He turned again to M.G. and said, "Wait here. Cover me." He handed her the flashlight. "Anything moves, you have my permission to blast away."

He got low to the floor and crawled inside, moving to his left away from the doorway. Still no shots were fired.

M.G. flipped on the flashlight, extending her arm to the doorway, pointing it straight ahead. She expected gunfire. There was none.

"I don't like this," Dano said. "Why the hell don't they shoot back?" He pointed his revolver towards the doorway and blasted away.

Again, there was no return fire.

Dano looked to M.G. She shined the light inside. It was quiet. Not a sound.

Her heart pounded. Her palms itched with sweat. She nodded to him.

He said, "Ladies first."

"Unh-uh, not tonight, Sir Lancelot. After you," she said, waving her Glock both toward him and the entrance. "Move it!"

He didn't like it, but he moved anyway.

M.G. shouted through the doorway, "We're coming in, Mick."

"Not yet," he shouted from the far end. He reached and picked up the lantern and held it high. "Okay, I'm ready."

Dano made a move toward the opening and ducked back behind the wall. M.G. smirked and said, "Move your ass!"

He turned toward the doorway and leaned in. Moving to his left as Mick did, he hugged the wall and crouched low.

M.G. shone the light through the opening and moved in to her right and stood erect. With one hand holding her weapon, she held the flashlight with the other.

Holding the light in front of her, she saw it, but couldn't say a word at first. Then, "Oh, shit."

She shone the light to the back wall. Mickey hung the lantern on a hook. His revolver was aimed at the temple of a big, shirtless man in cut-off jeans standing next to him.

M.G. aimed the light back to what she saw first, and gasped. Two rows of outrigger canoes sat erect on the floor. Inside each were dozens of skeletal warriors. They were posed as they would have appeared upon arrival, as if they were coming ashore. They were adorned with war-like ornate dress. Each one carried a spear.

Some of the warriors' mouths were open as if they were smiling. One of the canoes was slightly tipped, as if to replicate its movement on water.

But it was what was *on* that canoe that caused M.G. to gasp. A skeleton had one of those wide smiles as his spear jutted out, a fresh body impaled on it. Blood dripped down from the corpse, splattering the skull of the grinning skeleton. He'd won his last battle. Another body lay face down next to the outrigger canoe, a spear in its back.

M.G. stepped toward the tipped canoe in the middle of the chamber. The warriors had spilled to the listing side. She stood near the impaled body and put the light in it.

She heard it groan. Aiming the light on it, she saw it move. "We got a live one!" M.G. warned.

As Dano moved closer, M.G. asked him, "What do you think?"

He was caught in a whirl of emotions. Not knowing how to respond in the moment, he said nothing.

She looked to Mick. He responded by asking his hostage a question.

"Who are these people?" Lawai'a didn't respond. Putting the front of the gun barrel hard against his temple, Mick asked the same question again.

Lawai'a was shaking in fear, but answered quickly. "Lilia, she in charge. She da one on da spear. They fell in da darkness."

"'They'?" Mick asked.

"Ya, Lilia and Lio. Lio is a guard. Da breeder by Lio, he not hit. He on da floor, too."

"Dano!" Mick said, "Check the two on the floor."

Hesitating, Dano thought about ending it by shooting Lio. He knew that Mickey and M.G. were waiting for him to do something.

Cowering on the floor, the man begged for his life.

"Don't shoot. I don't want to die. I was just a breeder. I only took orders. Please don't shoo–"

A loud gunshot exploded from Dano's Glock, and Darrell Unsel Hartwig took a bullet to his lower spine. Paralyzed, he began pulling himself forward toward Dano using only his arms, begging for his life.

There was another loud blast from Dano's revolver. This time Darrell's head burst open. Blood, milky fluid, and gray matter spattered everywhere.

With his foot under the other man's shoulder, Dano pushed the body over as far as it would go.

Lio opened his eyes. They widened in recognition. "Dano. Get me to da boat." He breathed and then rolled back on his stomach. He whispered again, "Help me." Then Lio took his last gasping breath as his body went limp.

M.G. jerked toward Dano in shock. "How does he know you?"

"He doesn't," Dano snapped.

Lawai'a, who stood with a gun to his head, responded. "Why you here, Dano? Why you not with da boat?"

Panic set in. Instinctive reflexes took over. He pointed his revolver at Lawai'a and pulled the trigger again and again.

Intantly, M.G. fired her revolver as she stepped toward Dano, as did Mick. Lawai'a slumped to the floor. Mick fell on top of him. Dano was still standing. M.G. knelt on one knee before him, pushing the barrel of her Glock 17 under his crotch and pulled the trigger. The angle was just right: the bullet ripped upwards from his rectum, through his intestines, chest cavity, and out the top of his head.

"Just as I thought," she whispered. "Shit for brains."

Dano went down in a stinking heap. Blood boiled out from the exit hole near his right ear, spilling to the floor of the death cave. There he lay, in the chamber of the sacred burial grounds of his ancestors.

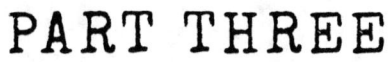

PART THREE

CHAPTER FORTY-ONE

8:17 AM - Ten Days Later

At the Hilo Medical Center on Waianuenue Avenue, M.G. stood in the hallway with Kat.

"... and he said that he wanted to be buried close to his high school buddy, Eddy Lord. The one who was in the engine room on the USS Arizona. They stayed in touch writing letters back then." Kat was cradling the wooden urn with his ashes inside. "Gordon's eardrums were broken, so the military wouldn't take him for the war."

M.G. took a deep breath before speaking. "I miss him too, Kat. He was a real inspiration to me. The EMTs said that he kept her protected until they arrived ... before his heart gave out."

Her voice cracked at the end. Kat gave her a one-armed embrace just as the door opened. A nurse stepped out of a room into the hallway and spoke with them.

"The young lady is ready and Mr. Zaugbum will be out shortly," she said.

"How's he doing?" Kat asked.

"He's such a flirt, he drives me nuts," the nurse replied with a laugh. "Anyway, his shattered ribs will heal and with physical therapy his arm should come around. The bullets tore him up pretty good. I hear you have a package to deliver?"

"Yeah," M.G. said. "We do."

***

In the VIP limo on the way back to Honolulu International Airport from Pearl Harbor, Mick and M.G. were going at it.

"On the plane he told me he got pissed with you," M.G. said, "because you called him *Gordo!*

"More than once," Mick admitted. "He splashed my wingtips at the airport. Revenge.

"Karma's a bitch. Back in Pine Nut, I nailed his new wellingtons with icy slush!"

The limo pulled to the curb at the airport terminal. Thomas J. Nachs got out first and opened the doors for the others.

"Thanks for setting up the ceremony at Pearl, Thomas," Mick said.

"No biggie, buddy. You'd do the same for me," he said. "Take care of the ladies. Aloha and *mahalo nui loa.*"

Kat wrinkled her brow. "I know 'aloha,' but–"

"*Mahalo nui loa* means thank you very much." He snapped his fingers, remembering something. "Let me guess, M.G. You or your buddies at Kurtistown homed in on Richard's GPS, am I right?"

"Yup," she said. "Gunderson got too cocky. He screwed up by bringing the GPS and radio signal with him. No matter what, we were going down that hole by the outhouse, regardless of what you guys came up with."

"What about your crazy Vietnam vet friend?" he asked.

"He got the weapons for us," she said, "Also, it turns out that Gunner handled FLOC's money in the Pacific. My Vietnam vet friend had him cuffed and handed over to the police on the Big Island."

"And he's gone?" Mick asked.

"Never got on the plane in Hilo. Had help, too," she added. "My family say he's somewhere near South Point, Maybe Discovery Harbour. A lot of *haoles* there."

"Going home now?" he asked, knowing the answer.

"Soon," she said. "My family's scouting things out down there as we speak. Another thing, Mick. That radio implant in Margaret's tooth–

she *wasn't* crazy. He was keeping tabs on her. Her husband, Polanski, had it done. He knew a guy who knew a dentist–something like that."

Mick shook his head and said, "She sure picked a couple of real losers for husbands."

M.G. poked him in the ribs. He flinched. "Oh, sorry!" she cried, "I forgot about your–"

"Ribs, yeah," he groaned, and then shrugged it off. "Maggie was his first female victim," he said, "the only one he didn't kill. In the end, it drove him crazy. That's why, in the cave, he slashed himself and not Bliss."

CHAPTER FORTY-TWO

11:11 PM CST September 3, 2001

At the airport in Capital City, They hailed a cab and headed to the Lutheran Hospital.

"Here we are," Kat said.

A woman watched from a third floor window as the group made its way to the hospital entrance.

"What do I say?" Bliss asked nervously.

"You don't have to say a word," Kat answered.

M.G. opened the door and Bliss stepped into the room.

"Oh, Mom," she said, her voice breaking, "You look so beautiful. I missed you so."

From the bed Maggie replied, "There's someone I want you to meet, and she's never met a female Marine before." She took Chloe's hand and pulled her close to the bedside. "Chloe, this is your sister, Bliss."

An Afterword from William

I'm glad you could join me for this caper. Having an audience helps make life (I mean, the afterlife) more interesting.

A guy just can't go around keeping all this to himself; he'd go crazy or something.

It's like when you're walking down the street and some homeless guy is carrying on, mumbling some crazy shit to–nobody. That's how I'd feel. If you weren't here, I mean.

Kathryn helped Chloe through her ordeal with Maggie regaining her consciousness and all.

My friend Gord-o is here with me. I ain't seen him, yet. But I will though, someday.

You might have recognized me. Old Curtis Miles Presley was me, and Pila–that was me, too. You see, the name Pila is Hawaiian for Bill and Bill is a nickname for William, but you already knew that.

Did I tell you that Ralphy quit speaking to me—directly, I mean? The old bugger gave up tryin' to change how I speak and crap like that. He still says I ain't refined enough–yet. I know he still likes me, but just the same, I piss him off. Not on purpose. It's just the way I go about things, it drives him crazy.

He has to go have a chat with God because of it. Then God reassigns him to other projects. I'm like the black sheep of the family.

If you read **"DIGGING UP BONES"**, you'd know how I got to be an angel and all of that nonsense. Then when I became one, Ralphy and Gabby (those head-honcho archangel guys) told me that there are different levels of angels.

A guy just can't up and get his wings. He has to practically jump through hoops, and crap like that. Plus you have to stay out of the way. Of course, that ain't me.

Sometimes a fucker gets me really pissed! I get myself involved. For that, I get into trouble and wind up getting an ass-chewin' from those guys.

Not God, though. God hardly ever gets angry. In fact I've never seen the old boy pissed off.

God doesn't yell–not at me, anyway. Seems like He lets it all be.

About the debate of God being a man or a woman ... what can I say, God is God. Men and women have tailbones. I don't think God ever had a tailbone. But that's me, though. I think different.

Someday, I'll get my wings, maybe.

Fini finis

P.S. Did I ever tell you about the grasshopper that walked into the bar? The bartender says, "Hey, we've got a drink named after you."

The grasshopper says, "Really? You got one named Ted?"

That just cracks me up.

Book I
DIGGING UP BONES
By
Augustus G Van Slyke

PSS: An FYI about my new friends. Back when I was growing up there was only one person who cared about folks like me, sheriff Gordon Maxwell. Today, it's a whole new ballgame.

We have friends now, lots of them, and they care about us. Check out these websites.

They are powerful people and righteous organizations looking out for kids like my friends and me. You can even be a member.

WWW.PROTECT.org. I have solid friends here like: Grier Week, Camille Cooper, JonAnn Glenhill, Jennifer Allen, and Lou Bank. These people are strong!

WWW.SNAPNETWORK.org. Check it out. Good people such as, Barbara Blaine, David Clohessy, and Barbara Dorris.

www.ingramcontent.com/pod-product-compliance
Lightning Source LLC
Chambersburg PA
CBHW070603130626
46556CB00001B/256